Purcell

Simon Mundy.

The Illustrated Lives of the Great Composers.

Purcell

Simon Mundy.

OMNIBUS PRESS

London/New York/Sydney

To John Mundy, my son

Cover design and art direction by Pearce Marchbank.
Cover photography by Julian Hawkins
Text design by BBB Design

Copyright © 1995 by Simon Mundy
This edition published in 1995 by Omnibus Press, a division of Book Sales Limited

ISBN 0.7119.4819.4
Order No.OP47751

Exclusive Distributors
Book Sales Limited,
8/9 Frith Street,
London W1V 5TZ, UK.

Music Sales Corporation,
257 Park Avenue South,
New York, NY 10010, USA.

Music Sales Pty Limited,
120 Rothschild Avenue,
Rosebery, NSW 2018, Australia.

To the Music Trade only:
Music Sales Limited,
8/9, Frith Street,
London W1V 5TZ, UK.

Special thanks are due to Nikki Russell for her exhaustive picture research
and to Jo Shapcott for casting an eye over the manuscript.

Illustration credits:Bankes Collection, Kingston Lacy (The National Trust) photograph The Courtauld Institute: 10;
Blaithwayt Collection, Dyrham Park (The National Trust) photograph The Courtauld Institute: 21; Bodleian Library,
Oxford: 41; Bridgeman Art Library: 72; By the permission of British Library: 63, 71, 73, 80, 87, 88, 92,108,144;
copyright British Museum: 146; private collection, photograph The Courtauld Institute: 109;
By Courtesy of the Dean and Chapter of Westminster: 17, 55, 78, 81, 82, 106, 136, 137,139, 148, 149, 150;
Denys Eyre Bauer Collection, Chiddingstone Castle, Kent: 36; Devonshire Collection, Chatsworth.
Reproduced by permission of the Chatsworth Settlement Trustees: 9; C. Masson & H-O.Brillouin /Enguerand: 121;
Mary Evans Picture Library: 14, 90, 103, 110; Fotomas Index: 77, 124; Garrick Club/E.T.Archive:128;
Hampshire Record Office: 76; Hulton Deutsch: 1; Peter Jackson: 4, 19, 62; The Peter Joslin Collection: 37, 56, 89;
Mansell Collection: 42, 46, 48, 83, 84, 118, 132; Museum of London: 16, 23, 24, 26, 27, 40, 50, 59, 74, 75, 99, 140;
National Portrait Gallery: frontispiece, 7, 12, 20, 51, 60, 64, 86, 97, 100, 122, 126, 129, 141; The Pilgrim Press Ltd, Derby:
57; Rex Features: 107, 113; The Royal College of Music: 70, 102; Sotheby's: 44, 53; Tate Gallery: 22; Theatre Museum,
V&A: 34, 116; Westminster City Archives: preface, 2, 15, 28, 31.

Printed in the United Kingdom by Staples Printers Limited, Rochester, Kent.

A catalogue record for this book is available from the British Library.

Contents

Preface

We know so much about 18th century composers like Bach and Handel that it comes as something as a shock to realise how little personal detail we have about Purcell. Even though he lived at a time when the Bank of England was being formed, John Evelyn was compiling his diary and many great libraries were being collected, we have precious few documents that are not the gleanings of official records; Treasury payments, church registers and the prefaces of the works published in or soon after his lifetime. We have hardly any letters from or to him: nothing that tells us about his love life and only one or two stories about his marriage and children. We know that his many pupils adored him, that he was good company if you met him in a tavern for an evening's drinking and that at court and in public concerts he was a performer who delighted audiences. But that is about all. Nonetheless Purcell's is a fascinating story. He lived entirely in London at the time when it first becomes recognisable as the city we know today. He knew everybody worth knowing; the politicians and playwrights, royalty and actors, poets and musicians. For nearly 20 years almost no national or royal occurrence happened without a Purcellian comment. He was also that rare figure, an artist who appealed to every sort of person, from the cleric buying his devotional songs, to the pompous Prince seeking homage or the well-oiled pub singer. He was as far from the romantic image of the composer cut off in the ivory tower of his art as it is possible to get. Perhaps above all Purcell's music is as much fun as it is glorious. This is a book, therefore, not about the minutiae of one man's life, nor about the intricacies of his music. It portrays instead the circumstances of that music and the events that shaped the man who wrote it. He died three hundred years ago but Henry Purcell can still be approached easily and with joy.

Simon Mundy, Gladestry, Radnor. July 1995.

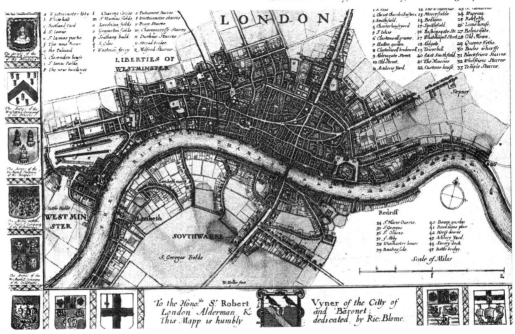

Chapter 1

The King being Come, the Scene Opened

'Mr. Crew saw me, and bid me come to his house and dine with him, which I did,' wrote Samuel Pepys in his diary on 21st February 1660, two days before his twenty-seventh birthday, 'and he very joyful told me that the House [of Commons] had made General Monk General of all the Forces in England, Scotland and Ireland...and that the House do intend to do nothing more than to issue writs and to settle a foundation for a free Parliament. After dinner I went back to Westminster Hall with him in his coach. Here I met with Mr. Lock and Pursell, Master of Musique, and went with them to the Coffee House, into a room next the water, by ourselves, where we spent an hour or two till Captain Taylor come and told us that the House had voted the gates of the City to be made up again and the members of the City that are in prison to be set at liberty...Here we had a variety of brave Italian and Spanish songs, and a canon for eight voices, which Mr. Lock had lately made on these words; "Domine salvum fac Regem". Here out of the window it was a most pleasant sight to see the city from one end to the other with a glory about it, so high was the light of the bonfires, and so thick round the City and the bells rang everywhere.'

A broadsheet illustration of a Coffee House scene. At that time dishes were used for drinking instead of handled mugs.

For Matthew Locke to have set the words *God Save the King* for singing in a coffee house (even in a private room) while the Parliament and the Army of the Commonwealth were locked in a power struggle was an act of some daring. At that moment nothing was inevitable. Charles Stuart was in Holland hoping that his bankrupt court in exile would soon have enough support to return to Britain. The rejoicing that Pepys, Locke, Silas Taylor and Mr. Purcell were watching had been sparked by the arrival of General Monck from his power base in Scotland. He brought with him disciplined soldiers to side with Parliament against the divided troops of various warlords who were intent on military rule and had been demanding money with menaces from the citizens because the system of taxation to pay wages had collapsed. Ten days earlier Locke and Pepys had gone for a drink together after meeting outside the Guildhall in the City to watch Monck emerge from a meeting with the Lord Mayor. They headed for the Star Tavern and made their way home to Westminster at about ten.

'The common joy that was everywhere to be seen! The number of bonfires, there being fourteen between St. Dunstan's and Temple Bar, and at Strand Bridge I could at one time tell thirty-one fires. In King Street seven or eight; and all along burning and roasting and drinking for rumps. There being rumps tied upon sticks and carried up and down. The butchers at the May Pole in the Strand rang a peal with their knives when they were going to sacrifice their rump. On Ludgate Hill there was one turning of the spit that had a rump tied upon it, and another basting of it. Indeed it was past imagination,

Bonfires and roasting rumps in the Strand by Temple Bar, 1660.

both the greatness and the suddenness of it. At one end of the street you would think there was a whole lane on fire, and so hot that we were fain to keep on the other side.'

The rumps of beef were being roasted to symbolize the demands for the dissolution of the Rump Parliament, which had been sitting with increasing illegitimacy and decreasing numbers throughout the Commonwealth period.

For musicians like Locke, a new order, preferably a Royalist one, could not come soon enough. Without a court or music in church, and with the theatres closed, there was no permanent employment around. Oliver Cromwell had provided some work for private and diplomatic purposes (as when Locke and his great friend from choirboy days at Exeter Cathedral, Christopher Gibbons, had been commissioned in 1653 to write the music for *Cupid and Death*, a masque to words by James Shirley, to greet the newly-arrived Portuguese ambassador). There was nothing that could be regarded as providing security and most musicians fell back on teaching or finding such work as was available in private houses. Locke had spent most of the decade alternating between London and Herefordshire where his wife and Silas Taylor lived.

Charles I's court had been a particularly generous one to musicians, with a Chapel Royal which was being enhanced to give the King some credibility in comparison with establishments on the continent. The need to compose lavish music for court masques (with their tentative glimpses across the channel to the new forms of Italian opera and French ballet) and the connected trend for more elaborate music in the thriving public theatres had all reinforced musicians' natural inclination against puritanism. Many, like Henry Cooke and William Lawes, had been active Cavaliers, fighting on the King's side (indeed William Lawes, England's finest composer of theatre music before Locke and Purcell, had died fighting as a member of the King's bodyguard at the Battle of Chester in 1645). For a few years after the King's execution in 1649 the royalist musicians laid low. The composer William Child, who had succeeded John Mundy as organist of St. George's Chapel in Windsor Castle, is said to have retired to a nearby farm. Child became an extraordinary symbol of continuity for 17th-century musicians. It is possible that he taught the elder Henry Purcell and his brother Thomas (one of which Pepys and Locke sang with in the coffee house) at Windsor and the younger

Purcell's supposed birthplace in St Anne's Lane, Westminster, from a sketch in 1845, a few years before it was pulled down. It is more likely that it was in fact his first marital home.

Henry Purcell studied his music at the Chapel Royal. Child outlived all of them. At 83 he played the organ at the coronation of William and Mary and died in 1697, aged 91.

We have no evidence that when Mr. Purcell joined Pepys and Locke on the night when General Monck was made Commander in Chief, he had a five month old baby, called Henry, at home. However, by piecing together dates from later in the young Henry's life it seems likely he was born in 1659 and possibly in September. The fact that we have no record may itself be an indication that it is a realistic date. That summer normal civil authority in England had all but collapsed as the Army, Parliament and Royalists vied for power. Parents were, in theory, required to register the birth of children with the civil authorities, as well as having them baptised. However many avoided it or arranged private baptisms, partly as a minor act of defiance against the Commonwealth, partly as a way of glossing over the exact shade of their religion, particularly if they were Catholics or had Catholic sympathies.

While Charles I was Defender of the (Anglican) Faith, his wife was a Catholic. The Royal Family in exile, having been helped to escape by English Catholics and maintained abroad by French ones, were inclined more or less openly to Catholicism, a fact which was to be at the basis of political instability for the rest of the century and half of the next. Musicians who needed to make a living close to the seat of power, whether it be royalist or republican, tended to keep their options open as far as was possible without putting their livelihoods in jeopardy. Matthew Locke, despite his Anglican cathedral upbringing in Exeter, was often accused of being a Catholic and may well have converted during his time abroad at the end of the Civil War. As a family the Purcells had connections with both religious branches, with Catholic members in Shropshire and Protestant ones in the Welsh borders, where John Purcell was elected as MP for Montgomeryshire in the 'free parliament' that Pepys had heard was to be called in early 1660. The Purcells in the Home Counties seem in general to have been on the Protestant side, which would makes sense if the elder Henry Purcell and his brother Thomas were brought up as choristers at Windsor. However their proximity to royalty all their lives meant that their positions reflected the ambiguities of the court. During the Commonwealth, despite its destructive puritanism, the state was of necessity more tolerant of different shades of religious opinion than the royal regimes (or more accurately the Parliaments with which they had to deal) before or after. After Oliver Cromwell's death in 1658 and the failure of his son Richard to install an hereditary Protectorate, the state was in no real position to enforce anything at all in a unified way. For people regarded as having suspicious politics – which certainly included those connected with music or the stage – ignoring the niceties of birth registration may well have been a quiet way of avoiding tiresome officials who had power but no real authority.

Whatever young Henry's parents' reasons for not officially marking his birth, it was a decision which has become extremely annoying to succeeding generations of biographers. Most recently writers have tended to side with John Hawkins and W.H.Cummings, writing in 1776 and 1903 respectively, that he was the son of Henry and Elizabeth Purcell. Sir Jack Westrup, writing in 1965, however, argued with passion that he was the son of Thomas and Katherine Purcell. Thomas was the elder Henry's brother. If they were the two boys brought up in Windsor, Thomas was three years younger and outlived Henry by 18 years, rising to highly influential positions at Charles II's court, both as a musician and as a member of the royal household. Sorting the evidence is not helped by the fact that as a family the Purcells had a habit of picking the same favourite names, particularly Edward, Henry and Katherine.

However there is a plausible sequence which makes Thomas the more likely father.

We know that young Henry's elder brother was Col. Edward Purcell because it says so on Edward's gravestone. Charles Purcell, who died at sea in 1686, named his brother Edward as his executor and refers to his mother, Katherine. Since Thomas Purcell's wife was called Katherine, the tree is complete. Thomas Purcell also referred to Henry as his son in a letter to the singer John Gostling on 8 February 1679.

'I have received ye favor of yours of ye 4th with ye incloseds for my sonne Henry: I am sorry we are like to be without you soe long as yours mentions: but tis very likely you may have a summons to appear among us sooner than you imagin: for my sonne is composing, wherein you will be chiefly concerned.'

It is also tempting to see the desolate anthem *Let Mine Eyes Run Down With Tears,* written about the time of Thomas's death in 1682, as a tribute to young Henry's father.

Just to confuse the matter it can be argued from the other side too, as Maureen Duffy does. The Charles Purcell who died in 1686 could have been referring to the Edward Purcell who lived as a gentleman at Mickleham, in Surrey, where his wife was daughter of the vicar – and there is no mention in Charles Purcell's will of the other young Purcells – Henry, Daniel and Joseph – which one might have expected had they been his brothers too. The advocates of the case for Henry being the son of Henry argue that the Surrey Edward and the Charles who died in 1686 were Thomas's sons and thus young Henry's first cousins. Henry's sons were therefore Col. Edward Purcell and the Charles Purcell who also died at sea, but while serving on board *The Tyger* in the vicinity of Barbados, in 1695 or '96. The letter from Thomas mentioning Henry as his son is then explained by the suggestion that Thomas either adopted his brother's children or acted as their guardian after their father's death in 1664 and was using the term 'sonne' loosely out of affection.

Neither hypothesis seems provable now and perhaps, while having his father alive or not through his childhood would have made a psychological difference to young Henry, a resolution is not so important. Father and uncle, whichever was which, were both musicians of considerable distinction. The family was a close one and Thomas made sure that young Henry had all the opportunities that a father in mid-17th century London could have wished.

In 1660 both Purcell brothers would have been struggling to make a living. Music was allowed but there were no public concert series then and musicians had to rely on private patronage or teaching. Cromwell had kept a few instrumental players on his payroll (partly because he liked to have music around him and partly for state events or semi-official ones, like the marriage of his daughter Frances, when an orchestra of 48 provided the dance music at the wedding feast) but there were no church posts for singers and many cathedral organs had been demolished.

Amid the general disorder, however, artists were tentatively pushing against the prohibition on theatres. Despite the continuation of the masque tradition for official celebrations by John Milton and James Shirley during the Commonwealth, anything that smacked of sheer entertainment was frowned upon. This was firmly enforced since so many of those connected with theatre and music were known royalists or suspected Catholics. None the less there was a moderate realisation, particularly by Milton who was the principal theorist of the Commonwealth, that the gifts of artists could transcend personal politics. A good example of this was Sir William D'Avenant, who had succeeded Ben Jonson as Poet Laureate in 1638. He claimed to be the illegitimate son of Shakespeare by the landlady of the Crown Inn in the Cornmarket at Oxford and he showed promise in his 'father's' old trade. At least one of D'Avenant's early plays *The Cruel Brother,* was staged in the Blackfriars Theatre, where Dryden tells us *The Tempest* was performed. D'Avenant fought for the Cavaliers and fled to Paris where he entered the service of Charles I's queen, Henrietta Maria. On a mission to England in 1650, though, he was arrested and is said to have been saved from execution by Milton.

Sir William D'Avenant (1606-1668), Poet Laureate, who claimed to be Shakespeare's illegitimate son and founded one of the two Patent theatre companies, The Duke's.

D'Avenant, once free again, remained in England and in the spring of 1656 decided to test whether Cromwell's toleration of music would extend to a form closer to the officially sanctioned masques. At first he moved cautiously, blurring the distinction between public and private performance by putting on *Declamations and Musick; after the manner of the Ancients* in a room seating four hundred (but only attracting one hundred and fifty) people at the back of Rutland House in Aldersgate Street, where he lived. The performance, a series of dialogues just about as tedious and devoid of theatrical instinct as the censors could wish, had musical interludes by Henry Lawes (William's surviving brother), Henry Cooke and George Coleman, an erstwhile member of Charles I's Chapel Royal. Coleman's brother Edward and his sister-in-law Catherine took the acting parts – in itself provocative since one of the prime complaints of Parliament against the Stuart court had been sparked by the appearance of women on stage. D'Avenant himself recognised that the experiment was less than riveting — and a long way from his ambitious but failed attempt to found an English Opera House in 1639 – as he made clear in the Prologue to the *Declamations:-*

Think this your passage, and the narrow way
To our Elisian Field, the Opera:
Tow'rds which some say we have gone far about,
Because it seems so long since we set out.

D'Avenant, who had seen proper opera in Paris, was well aware that he was presenting a milk and water version but, even if the room was not half full on the first night, he was encouraged enough to continue with a run of ten performances. The reaction of the authorities must have been positive because a few months later D'Avenant was able to push the boundaries back much further. There was still no question of presenting anything that looked too like the plays with music that had been the staple fare at the Blackfriars Theatre in the 1630s.

Fully-fledged opera, with recitative instead of spoken dialogue, had never been tried, however, and by adopting language in describing the new venture which steered away from normal theatrical convention, D'Avenant hoped to sidestep the puritan restrictions. So *The Siege of Rhodes,* as this first English Opera was called, was divided into five 'entries' instead of acts. He avoided the term opera too, calling the evening *A Representation by the Art of Prospective in Scenes and the Story sung in Recitative Musick,* which was hardly snappy but gave him some cover. Despite the fact that he commissioned ambitious scenery from John Webb – who had been the great Inigo Jones's assistant, making the working drawings from Jones's sketches for the court masques – D'Avenant still did not dare to risk staging *The Siege of Rhodes* in a properly equipped theatre at first and persevered with the inconvenient and low-ceilinged room in Rutland House.

'It has been often wisht,' he wrote in the preface to the printed edition of the script, 'that our scenes (we having obliged ourselves to the variety of five changes, according to the ancient drammatick distinctions made for time) had not been confined to eleven foot in height, about fifteen in depth, including the places of passage reserv'd for the musick. This is so narrow an allowance for the fleet of Solyman the Magnificent, his army, the Island of Rhodes, and the varieties attending the siege of the city, that I fear you will think we invite you to such a contracted trifle as that of the Caesars carved upon a nut.'

Less than perfect it may have been but for the show-starved Londoners *The Siege of Rhodes* was a wonderful indication that something like normal life was returning. The opera was a huge success. Just as importantly though, it brought together much of the musical talent then in London for some public work. As in the *Declamations*, D'Avenant called on a pot-pourri of composers, allowing the script and scenery to be the unifying factors instead of the music as would have been normal practice in an opera in Italy. This may have been a matter of time but it may also have been a political expedient to spread the responsibility for the work as far as possible in case there was any trouble. So Henry Lawes wrote the first and last 'entries', Matthew Locke the fourth, Henry Cooke the second and third and there were instrumental interludes and dances by Charles Coleman and George Hudson. Cooke took the part of Solyman, Locke was the Admiral, Edward and Catherine Coleman appeared and Henry Purcell was Mustapha.

The success of *The Siege of Rhodes* was greater than D'Avenant had expected but the work plainly ran into some trouble with the government since nothing further was produced for two years. Even though Cromwell's death in the meantime had

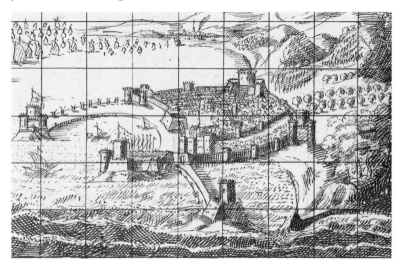

John Webb's design
for the stagecloth for
The Siege of Rhodes, 1656.

The young Thomas Betterton as Solyman in an early 1660s revival of *The Siege of Rhodes*.

weakened the government's grip, his son Richard was sufficiently disturbed to order an inquiry into D'Avenant's activities in 1658. While there seem to have been no serious consequences from this investigation, in D'Avenant's next attempt to return to the stage, *The Cruelty of the Spaniards in Peru*, he left out his one female performer and reverted to a rather less overtly dramatic format. He was, though, able to move out of the confines of Rutland House. The Blackfriars Theatre had, sadly, been demolished a short while before in 1655. The other indoor theatre from the 1620s, The Phoenix (or The Cockpit as it had originally been called and as it was still often referred to) in Drury Lane was usable and indeed had been used throughout the Commonwealth by troupes of actors prepared to risk arrest by putting on unlicensed performances; hit-and-run players, one might call them.

D'Avenant, though, did not want his shows broken up by soldiers and so he moved more cautiously. But by 1659 the political situation was sufficiently anarchic for him to feel that he was unlikely to be stopped. So he moved forward again into more dramatic material with *The History of Sir Francis Drake* (as in the previous piece, being rude about the Spanish was always likely to appeal to the politicians) and revived *The Siege of Rhodes* in a more substantial form, together with a sequel, and staged them all at The Cockpit. For Londoners it meant that there was something approaching a full season of legal entertainment for the first time in 17 years, since Parliament had demanded the closure of the theatres in 1642. For musicians like the Colemans and the Purcells it meant nearly continuous work in front of the public with a good chance of being paid; a situation almost as astonishing.

For some, even those who had disapproved most strongly of the Commonwealth, like the diarist John Evelyn, the whole enterprise seemed uncomfortably frivolous at a time when a renewal of civil war was highly likely, as he noted on 5 May 1659, when he went:-

'...to see a new opera, after the Italian way, in recitative music and scenes, much inferior to the Italian composure and magnificence; but it was prodigious that in a time of such public consternation such a vanity should be kept up, or permitted. I, being engaged with company, could not decently resist the going to see it, though my heart smote me for it.'

Evelyn was one of the few people in the audience who had seen real opera in Rome and D'Avenant was lucky that his rather sniffy response was unrepresentative. Tragically none of the music from any of D'Avenant's operas has survived – or at least can be identified – except one dance by Locke from *Sir Francis Drake*, which was published 20 years later.

By the spring of 1660 it was clear that there was unlikely to be a workable agreement among the anti-monarchy factions in the country and that General Monck was inclining towards

General George Monck (1608-1670), the Commander-in-Chief of the Commonwealth Army who invited Charles Stuart to return to Britain as King in 1660.

allowing Charles Stuart back into Britain. A steady stream of people were now crossing the channel to Breda in the Dutch Republic, where Charles was quietly building up his household and an alternative administration. A new House of Commons was elected on 25 April and the House of Lords, which had been abolished in 1649, was allowed by Monck to assemble again. Charles had already forwarded to Monck letters to be read to Parliament, including the Declaration of Breda, in which – at Monck's suggestion – Charles promised solutions to most of the issues which had had the Army and the House of Commons at each other's throats for the previous year: a pardon for all except those who had signed his father's death warrant or participated in his execution, confirmation of land titles exchanged since the Civil War, the payment of the Army's back pay and freedom of conscience in religion. As is the way with political promises, all of them were eroded to a greater or lesser extent over the coming years but the Declaration was astute enough to ensure that Charles was acceptable as King to all but ardent republicans.

Among those making their way to Charles was Sir William D'Avenant, who crossed in March 1660 (no doubt anxious to be confirmed in the post of Poet Laureate he had held in the last reign). His fellow playwright and future rival as a theatrical manager, Thomas Killigrew, was already there, installed as a Groom of the Bedchamber and the last official King's Jester. Pepys crossed with Sir Edward Montagu, the Admiral of the Fleet, to whom he was Secretary, ready to bring Charles back. Pepys first met Charles on 17 May at The Hague and found him 'a very sober man'. It is an interesting first impression but well wide of the mark as Pepys soon admitted when he got to know him better on the voyage to Dover. Thomas Purcell possibly made the journey to the Hague too, since he was made Groom of the Robes in Ordinary (a similar post to Killigrew's) almost a month before Charles returned to England. It was a position which kept the Purcells at the heart of court life and set the family pattern for two generations. Until the death of Queen Anne in 1714 there was never a time when there was not a Purcell close to the Crown in some capacity.

Charles Stuart landed at Dover, where he was received by Monck, on 25 May and entered London as Charles II on 29 May, his thirtieth birthday. The city, which as we have seen above, had been anticipating the event for several months, excelled itself in celebrations, which must have been especially sweet after the austere years of Cromwellian rule. Charles arrived, as John Evelyn, observed,

'...with a triumph of above 20,000 horse and foot, brandishing their swords, and shouting with inexpressible joy; the ways strewed with flowers, the bells ringing, the streets hung with tapestry, fountains running with wine; the Mayor, Aldermen, and all the Companies, in their liveries, chains of gold, and banners; Lords and Nobles, clad in cloth of silver, gold and velvet; the windows and balconies, all set with ladies; trumpets, music, and myriads of people flocking, even so far as from Rochester, so they were seven hours in passing the city, even from two in the afternoon till nine at night.'

The music may well have been Matthew Locke's best known piece today; his *Musick for His Majesties Cornets and Sackbutts.*

Three weeks later, on 16 June, Charles re-formed the Chapel Royal and during that and the following month he announced the rest of his permanent musical establishment. Some of those that had held places under his father were retained but inevitably the intervening years had made gaps in their ranks and there were many replacements in the 48 appointments. Among them Matthew Locke took the place of John Coperario as composer and Henry Lawes that of Thomas Ford, while Henry Purcell Snr. was named as assistant singer and lutenist to the nonegenarian Angelo Notari. Born in 1566, two years after Shakespeare, Notari had left Venice for the court of James I in 1610, a little before Monteverdi had moved to the city, and so for English composers of the middle part of the century he represented an important link with the mannerist Italian madrigal tradition and the earliest stages of the baroque. For Henry Purcell, however, it meant that in 1660 he did the work and Notari collected the pay. Thomas Purcell was made a Gentleman of the Chapel Royal, singing tenor.

One appointment which was to be of considerable significance to the younger Henry Purcell was that of John Hingston, who in July was made Tuner and Repairer of His Majesty's Wind Instruments. Hingston, who may have been Purcell's godfather, was one of the few musicians who had held an official position under the Protectorate. He had been Organist to Cromwell at Hampton Court, leader of his small permanent band and music tutor to his daughters. Cromwell had also required Hingston to oversee the boys he retained to sing. There were, however, only two of them and, thanks to the disbanding of church choirs and choir schools, Hingston had trouble recruiting even them – as he made clear to Cromwell in 1656:-

'Many of the skilfull professors of the said Science [of Musick] have during the laste Warrs and troubles dyed in want and there being now noe preferrment or Encouragement in the way of Musick no man will breed his Child in it...'

The position four years later was no better. The job of putting the choirs back together fell to Henry Cooke (usually known by his Royalist forces rank as Captain Cooke) at the Chapel Royal and, in February 1661, Henry Purcell senior at Westminster Abbey. For both Masters of the Choristers the first few months were spent in talent spotting. According to Matthew Locke, for the first year the treble parts in the Chapel music had to be supplied or supported by cornetts, wooden wind instruments that were like a cross between oboes and trumpets. Henry Purcell was also made the first Music Copyist at Westminster Abbey (a job young Henry was later to inherit). He was faced with a major undertaking since many of the singing books containing the

Westminster Abbey from the North before the addition of Hawksmoor's towers. The porch has been demolished.

music for the services were destroyed in the Civil War.

Unlike previous and future holders of his post, Cooke had no cathedral choirs from which to poach. For any boy in England with a half-decent voice 1660 could have been a year of easy auditions. Cooke needed an establishment of 12 boys for the Chapel Royal and his first finds included some notable names; Pelham Humfrey, who was to be his son-in-law and successor, John Blow – who may have been in a group of five boys that Cooke brought back from Newark and Lincoln – and Michael Wise, from Salisbury.

Once the Westminster choirs, at Whitehall Palace and the Abbey, were in place the main objective was to be prepared for Charles's coronation, set for 23 April 1661. For all the royal musicians and those employed by the city livery companies, the days surrounding the coronation must have been exhausting. Three days before it Charles created or upgraded several Peers in the splendour of Inigo Jones's Banqueting House (the most modern and now the only remaining part of Whitehall Palace), his Lord Chancellor, Edward Hyde, being made Earl of Clarendon. Then the King and his brother James went off to the Cockpit to see a production (not a very good one, according to Pepys) of Beaumont and Fletcher's *The Humorous Lieutenant*. The bachelor King took along his mistress, 20-year-old Barbara Palmer, 'with whom', Pepys rather primly remarked given that they had been lovers for a year, 'the King do discover a great deal of familiarity.'

Plans of the Cockpit or Phoenix Theatre. Dating from 1617 it was one of the earliest indoor theatres in London and became the main venue for plays at the Restoration.

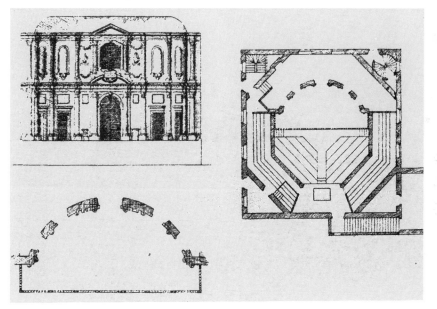

On 22 April the City of London paid its homage to Charles as he processed in a cavalcade from Tower Hill to Whitehall. Pepys with Sir William Penn (of Pennsylvania fame) watched from a room well stocked with 'wine and good cake' at a flag-maker's on Cornhill. The procession was not a cheap affair of which to be a part. Evelyn described it as 'exceeding rich'and Pepys, who claimed that his eyes were 'overcome' by the gold and silver, was told later that night by the Earl of Sandwich that his suit for the occasion had been made in France at a cost of £200, the equivalent of many thousands today.

The coronation service itself began in Westminster Abbey the next morning at 11.00am. The service was as sumptious as the previous evening's cavalcade had been. The musicians had specially bought liveries and besides the two choirs, which may have been placed separately in the Abbey for antiphonal effect, the King's ensemble of 24 violins (formed in imitation of Louis XIV's group in Paris) was augmented by wind instruments, trumpets and organs – the last presumably installed for the occasion since Westminster Abbey's organ had been damaged by Cromwell's soldiers in the Civil War. The choirs performed

Souvenir mugs for sale in London to mark the Coronation of Charles II in April 1660.

'anthems and rare music', said Evelyn, some of it by Henry Cooke, Henry Lawes and William Child. However, much of the late night practice Cooke had demanded from his singers – and Henry Purcell's absence from the cavalcade the day before – was wasted on the crowd of spectators ranged on scaffolding on the north side of the Abbey, as Pepys made clear,

'...a General Pardon also was read by the Lord Chancellor, and medalls flung up and down by my Lord Cornwallis, of silver, but I could not come by any. But so great a noise that I could make but little of the musique; and indeed it was lost to everybody.'

Outside the Abbey too scaffolding had been erected so that 10,000 people could watch the newly crowned King process to Westminster Hall for the coronation banquet, in itself a superb piece of theatre with the Knights of the Bath carrying the first course to high table preceded by Lords Suffolk, Northumberland and Ormonde on horseback and, after dinner, the King's Champion riding in to fling down the gauntlet and challenge any 'to deny Charles Stuart to be lawful King of

England'. For those people not seated at the tables, finding some food was a bit of a free-for-all. However Pepys was happy enough. 'I took a great deal of pleasure to go up and down, and look upon the ladies, and to hear the musique of all sorts, but above all the 24 violins.' The number was worth noting. Charles I's orchestra had only been a band of 14 violins.

Charles II's enthusiasm for music meant that composers, players and singers were kept busy. They not only sang the services at Whitehall Palace, they entertained the royal

One of the triumphal arches set up in London to welcome Charles II at his restoration.

family in private and provided background music at public events, under the supervision of Nicholas Lanier as Master of the King's Musick. (Lanier had held the post since Charles I's succession in 1625, had written the music to many of Ben Jonson and Inigo Jones's masques and toured Italy buying pictures for the royal collection, many of which are still in England.) Sometimes a single singer accompanied himself on the lute, as the elder Henry Purcell would have done standing in for the aged Notari; sometimes a small group, after 1662 formalised into a specialist chamber ensemble under the direction of John Banister, from the 24 violins performed; sometimes a consort of voices. Charles's tastes were eclectic, though he seems to have preferred strings to wind instruments and trumpets, but for ceremonial occasions there was a Kettle Drummer, and 16 trumpeters under Jervaise Price, the Sergeant Trumpeter. Eight of them were despatched to Portugal to accompany Charles's 23-year-old bride, Catherine of Braganza, to Portsmouth in 1662. Gradually the King introduced a fashion for having anthems in the Chapel Royal accompanied by the strings as well as organ continuo. Unlike churches and indeed monarchs now, he had a permanent string orchestra in his employ; so why not use them?

With the deaths of Henry Lawes and Angelo Notari in 1662 there were more posts available for the Purcell brothers. Henry senior formally took over the work he had been doing for some time and Thomas was given Lawes' job as Composer for the lutes and voices. Good jobs these may have been but the salaries were less than generous and included many necessary expenses. The basic pay for a Gentleman of the Chapel Royal was £40 per year, an amount that had changed little in 40 years. This plainly did not go far enough, as the Gentlemen complained in September 1662 when they petitioned the King, pointing out that £40 in the reign of James I was the equivalent of £80 under Charles II. The Steward of the Household reviewed the matter and, as is the way with wage claims, settled on the rather lower figure of £70. On top of this Thomas Purcell received £32 2/6d for his composer's post, but half of that went to pay for his livery, 'a camlet [wool and silk] gown, garded with black velvet and furred'.

Extra fees were to be had when the musicians needed to leave London, either going with the King on his summer excursions to

Windsor and Newmarket, where the King rode in the races as well as watching them, or for duties such as greeting the new Queen on her arrival at Portsmouth. Being awarded the pay was one thing: extracting it from the King's Treasury, however, was quite another. While this made a life of credit the norm, it did have the advantage of forcing the court musicians to be active in the main musical life of London – in the churches, tavern music-rooms (where there was no entrance fee but the expectation of generous tips) and the theatres.

For the first few years after Charles's restoration theatre life was abundant. At the old Cockpit in Drury Lane John Rhodes

Catherine of Braganza (1638-1705), the Portuguese Princess whom Charles II married in 1662.

replaced D'Avenant. William Beeston, an old adversary of D'Avenant's whose father had built the Cockpit in 1617, opened up the Salisbury Court Theatre. Dating from 1629, this was the last of the theatres to be built before the Restoration. It was shared over the next few years with George Jolly, who had taken his company to tour Germany during the interregnum. D'Avenant himself used Salisbury Court too but recruited a new company of actors (among them the young Thomas Betterton, whom he poached from Rhodes) and converted a tennis Court in Portugal Row, off Lincoln's Inn Fields, into a theatre which he named The Duke's.

Killigrew had also set up his own company in another converted tennis court just round the corner in Clare Market, and the rivalry, which was to become ever more bitter and to dominate London theatre life for the next 20 years, was soon evident. They fought with each other and with Sir Henry Herbert, the Master of the Revels, who was nominally in charge of them. The King suggested, rather idiotically, that they might get along better if their companies amalgamated. They did not merge well and were soon in hot competition, as two observations by Pepys, noted two days apart in July 1661, show clearly.

On 2 July, only a few days after its opening, Pepys went to D'Avenant's theatre in Lincoln's Inn Fields:-

Elizabeth of Bohemia (1596-1662), Charles II's aunt, at whose marriage Shakespeare's *The Tempest* was performed in 1613.

'...to Sir William D'Avenant's Opera; this being the fourth day that it hath begun, and the first that I have seen it. Today was acted the second part of *The Siege of Rhodes*. We staid a great while for the King and Queen of Bohemia,' [the King's aunt Elizabeth – for whose wedding celebrations in 1613 fourteen plays including Shakespeare's *The Tempest* were performed and who had just returned to London for her few remaining months after nearly fifty years in exile: her life was like Miranda's in reverse; an incredible beauty who married a foreign prince and then wandered Europe, usurped ironically by a prince named Ferdinand]. 'And by the breaking of a board over our heads, we had a great deal of dust fall into the ladies' necks and the men's haire, which made good sport. The King being come, the scene opened; which indeed is very fine and magnificent, and well acted, all but the Eunuche, who was so much out that he was hissed off the stage.'

On 4 July Pepys tried a play of Killigrew's, a revival from pre-Civil War days:-

'I went to the theatre and there I saw *Claracilla* (the first time I saw it), well acted. But strange to see this house, that used to be so thronged, now empty since the Opera begun; and so will continue for a while, I believe.'

The battle between D'Avenant and Killigrew was institutionalised when in 1662 Charles granted patents to them both, licensing their companies and thus excluding Rhodes, Jolly and Beeston. Killigrew responded by renaming his company The

King's Servants and building a theatre, dubbed the Theatre Royal, on a old riding yard at the corner of Drury Lane and Bridges Street (now Kemble St.). It cost £1,500 to construct and opened on 7 May 1663 with *The Humourous Lieutenant,* the Beaumont and Fletcher play that Charles had been to see a

Thomas Killigrew (1612-1683), playwright, the last King's Jester and founder of the Theatre Royal, Drury Lane.

couple of days before his coronation. Killigrew had the rights to all Beaumont and Fletcher's plays as well as Ben Jonson's and about six of Shakespeare's, including *Othello, The Merry Wives of Windsor* and *A Midsummer Night's Dream.* D'Avenant, on the other hand, had *The Tempest, Romeo and Juliet, Hamlet* and *King Lear* in his care. A French visitor said the Theatre Royal, Drury Lane was the best equipped theatre he had ever seen. The whole building, though, would have fitted onto the stage of the present Theatre Royal. The patent from the King made Killigrew's company part of the royal household, with liveries of Grooms of the Bedchamber in recognition of their manager's rank – the scarlet and gold which stage footmen, as the successors to the members of the patent companies, at Drury Lane and Covent Garden still wear. Oranges could be bought from Mrs. Meggs or one of her assistants, but only in the better seats.

One far-reaching condition of the theatres' charter was that women's parts were to be played by women, a demand argued on moral grounds that turned on its head the previous justification for using boy actors:-

'And for as much as many plays formerly acted do contain several profane obscene and scurrilous passages and the womens' parts therein have been acted by men in the habit of women at which some have taken offence, for the preventing of these abuses for the future

Margaret Hughes (d. 1719), Prince Rupert's mistress and the first actress to play Desdemona. Painted by Sir Peter Lely.

we do...give leave that all the womens' parts to be acted in either of the said two Companies for the time to come may be performed by women so long as these recreations which by reasons of the abuses aforesaid were scandalous and offensive, may by such reformation be esteemed not only harmless delights but useful and instructive representations of human life to such of our good subjects as shall resort to the same.'

Killigrew tested the boundaries of the new licence to the full when, in October 1664, he revived his 1640 play, *The Parson's Wedding*, with an entirely female cast. Such ambitious and innovative projects meant that for the first time in English theatre there was an urgent need for good actresses. Rebecca Marshall (and her sister Anne), Margaret Hughes (the first female Desdemona and later mistress of Prince Rupert) and Catherine Coleman took major roles but Killigrew realised he had to train new talent. He responded by starting London's first acting school at the Barbican. Nonetheless Killgrew must have felt he was taking a big risk when, in the spring of 1665, he accepted the advice of his leading man, Charles Hart, and promoted to the stage from the job of orange-seller a 15-year-old girl called Nell Gwynne. She was given the part of Cydaria (the name possibly a pun on cider, alluding to Nell's birth in Hereford), the young daughter of Montezuma, opposite Hart, as Cortez, in Dryden's tragedy *The Indian Emperor*. It was not an auspicious start for, within a few weeks, the theatres had closed and people were leaving London as quickly as they could to escape the plague.

One of the hooded figures who preceded the plague wagons through the streets in 1665.

Chapter 2

In Ordinary, without Fee

The elder Henry Purcell did not enjoy the court position he had inherited from Notari at the end of 1663 for long. On 11 August 1664 he died and two days later he took his sad place among the other musicians in the cloisters of Westminster Abbey. He was only 40 and died without leaving a will. At the turn of the year

The catalogue of a bad plague week in London. One person died of lethargy, three of fright, but 7,165 of plague. Only four parishes were clear of the disease.

The Diseases and Casualties this Week.

Abortive—	
Aged—	43
Ague—	2
Apoplexie—	1
Bleeding—	2
Burnt in his Bed by a Candle at St. Giles Cripplegate—	1
Canker—	1
Childbed—	42
Chrisomes—	18
Consumption—	134
Convulsion—	64
Cough—	2
Dropsie—	33
Feaver—	309
Flox and Small-pox—	5
Frighted—	3
Gowt—	1
Grief—	3
Griping in the Guts—	51
Jaundies—	5

Imposthume—	11
Infants—	16
Killed by a fall from the Belfrey at Alhallows the Great—	1
Kingsevil—	2
Lethargy—	1
Palsie—	1
Plague—	7165
Rickets—	17
Rising of the Lights—	11
Scowring—	5
Scurvy—	2
Spleen—	1
Spotted Feaver—	101
Stilborn—	17
Stone—	2
Stopping of the stomach—	9
Strangury—	1
Suddenly—	1
Surfeit—	49
Teeth—	121
Thrush—	5
Timpany—	1
Tissick—	11
Vomiting—	3
Winde—	3
Wormes—	15

Christned { Males — 95 / Females — 81 / In all —— 176 }   Buried { Males —— 4095 / Females —— 4202 / In all —— 8297 }   Plague — 7165

Increased in the Burials this Week —————— 607

Parishes clear of the Plague — 4   Parishes Infected —— 126

The Assize of Bread set forth by Order of the Lord Maior and Court of Aldermen; A penny Wheaten Loaf to contain Nine Ounces and a half, and three half-penny White Loaves the like weight.

Elizabeth Purcell and her children moved from the lodgings that had been tied to Henry's mastership of the choristers into a house a short walk away in Tothill Street. Henry's court post of lutenist was taken by John Goodgroome, his Abbey job by Thomas Blagrave, with whom he had shared the part of Mustapha in the revivals of *The Siege of Rhodes*. Henry's death left his brother Thomas head of the family and for the following decade he would have had to be the father figure for all the Purcell children.

When the plague struck a few months later in May 1665 the court – along with its musicians – was quick to move away from London and Westminster. First it journeyed a few miles up river to Hampton Court (where the schoolroom was improved to cope with Henry Cooke's Chapel Royal boys), then, when disease seemed again too close for comfort, much farther away to Salisbury. Even there people were not completely safe. However the conditions were much better than in the fetid streets of London during a particularly hot and windless summer. They were wise to leave. The plague began in Covent Garden and St Giles-in-the-Fields and soon moved along Holborn and around the theatres to the Strand. In one week in September 12,000 people died. Doctors and apothecaries not only had no answers to the plague, they themselves were almost entirely wiped out. It was not until the frost of winter had killed off the fleas carrying the disease that the inhabitants began to face the future with any confidence. But by Christmas, when most of those who had taken to the country came back, around 100,000 people, a third of the metropolitan population, had died. It was not considered sensible for the King to return until February, though the Purcells seem to have been confident enough to be in London by January when Thomas's son William was born and baptised at St Mary-le-Strand, an area which had been at the heart of the plague district a few months earlier.

By the summer of 1666, another exceptionally hot one, life was back to something like normal. But the fear of plague still lingered and the insecurity was not helped by the start of a particularly disastrous naval war with the Dutch. This, perhaps the first imperial trade war that England fought, was pointless on all counts. It meant the appearance of press gangs who, on the authority of the Lord Mayor of London, Sir Thomas Bludworth ('a silly fellow', Pepys called him), grabbed men at random, flung them into gaol and then sent them to sea. Officials of the navy like Pepys were disgusted but, because of the shortage of genuine recruits, powerless to stop it. The

The Great Fire of London on 3 September 1666, seen from the river under the arches of London Bridge. The old St Paul's Cathedral stands about to be engulfed.

Dutch wars cost thousands of lives and destroyed the reputation of Charles and his government. The euphoria that had greeted his coronation was long spent.

For once London, and even the court, was in a sober mood. The Duke's Theatre remained closed until 29 October, when D'Avenant revived a production from the 1664 season; Sir George Etherege's first play, *The Comical Revenge* or *Love in a Tub*. Killigrew waited until 7 December when he reopened the Theatre Royal with one of his best properties, *The Maid's Tragedy* by Beaumont and Fletcher. The next night he gave Nell Gwynne another part, as the widow Lady Wealthy (hardly typecasting for a 16-year-old) in a new comedy called *The English Monsieur*. It was by James Howard, one of Dryden's less talented brothers-in-law, who became notorious for giving *Romeo and Juliet* a happy ending. Killigrew's attendances were well down, however, as he complained to Pepys two months later. It is hardly surprising, given that after the plague had come the Great Fire in September 1666.

On the night of 2 September Thomas Farrinor, baker to the king, went to bed at ten, having, he thought, put out the fire in his oven but leaving a pile of sticks close to it. It was a Saturday night. Three hours later the house in Pudding Lane was full of smoke and he escaped across the roof with his wife, daughter and manservant. The maid was not so lucky. At first it seemed no worse than a minor outbreak and the city authorities were not alarmed. A strong easterly wind, however, blew the flames into a neighbouring inn and by early on Sunday morning

300 houses were on fire, including those at the city end of London Bridge. There was little fire-fighting equipment and people seemed to be more intent on evacuating their goods than stopping the flames. Pepys went to the King and the Duke of York who ordered houses to be pulled down to form fire breaks and offered soldiers to do it. But when Pepys eventually found the exhausted Bludworth, the Lord Mayor answered dispiritedly that people would not obey him, 'I have been pulling down houses but the fire overtakes us faster than we can do it.' Nonetheless many did what they could. Those at court, including the King and his brother, worked side by side with the citizens and the Dean of Westminster led the Abbey choristers to help. By the time the wind died down and the fire was stopped at midnight the following Wednesday almost all of the city within the old walls and a swathe of riverfront from the Fleet to the Temple was destroyed.

Of the 80,000 people made homeless, 20,000 never returned to London. Most of the city's landmarks disappeared, among them St.Paul's Cathedral (which Wren had been advising the

Sir Christopher Wren's unrealised £7m plan for rebuilding London; a similar layout to modern Manhattan.

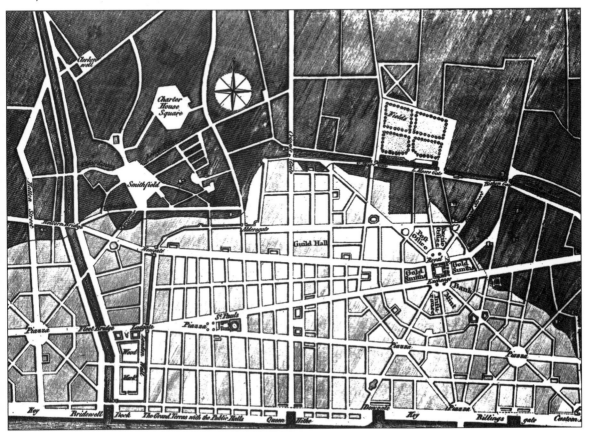

27

Samuel Pepys (1633-1703), diarist for nine years, Secretary to the Navy Board and President of the Royal Society. The autograph is from a letter of 1670.

Dean on restoring only six days before the fire), the old theatre in Salisbury Court and Baynard's Castle, the Norman palace rebuilt by Henry VII as his city residence and home to the wives of Henry VIII. But the walls of the Guildhall survived (and underneath them the city archives) and the fire never reached the Tower. In two years the financial centre of the country and the largest city in Europe had been destroyed; its buildings reduced to rubble so thick the street level was raised by four feet and its population temporarily shrunk by disease and emigration to little more than a third of its pre-plague figure. Sir Christopher Wren delivered a plan to the King within a week of the fire for a new city built on modern neo-classical lines and John Evelyn sketched one too. Parliament and the City Corporation baulked at the estimated cost of over £7m, however, and the property rights of freeholders proved impossible to dislodge. London gradually re-emerged on the old street plan with only Wren's churches giving a clue as to how his baroque city might have looked.

There is a fascinating account in Pepys's diary (12 February 1667) of the hopes and fears that Killigrew had in the months following the fire. It describes the difficulties he faced but also his determination to make his company part of the mainstream of European music theatre – and it highlights the differences between the state of theatre life in Charles I's time and Charles II's.

'With my Lord Brouncker by coach to his house, there to hear some Italian musique: and here we met Tom Killigrew, Sir Robert Murray and the Italian Signor Baptista [Giovanni Baptista Draghi – one of the Queen's music staff at Somerset House] who hath proposed a play in Italian for the opera which T. Killigrew do intend to have up; and here he [Draghi] did sing one of the acts. He himself is poet as well as the musician; which is very much, and he did sing the whole from the words without any musique prickt, and played all along upon a Harpsicon most admirably, and the composition most excellent. The words I did not understand, and so know not how they are fitted, but believe very well, and all in the recitative very fine...T. Killigrew and Sir R. Murray, who understood the words, did say most excellent. I confess I was mightily pleased with the musique. He pretends not to voice, though it be good but not excellent. This done, T. Killigrew and I to talk; and he tells me how the audience at his house is not above half so much as it used to be before the late fire. That Knipp [Mary Knepp] is like to make the best actor that ever come upon the stage, she understanding so well: that they are going to give her £30 a year more. That the stage is now by his pains a thousand times better and more glorious than ever heretofore. Now wax-candles, and many of them; then not above 3lbs of tallow: now all things civil, no rudeness anywhere; then, as in a bear-garden: then two or three fiddlers, now nine or ten of the best: then nothing but rushes upon the ground, and everything else mean; now all otherwise: then the Queene seldom and the King never would come; now not the King only for state, but all civil people do think they may come as well as any. He tells me that he hath gone several times (eight or ten times, he tells me) hence to Rome to hear good musique; so much he loves it, though he did never sing or play a note. That he hath ever endeavoured in the late King's time and in this to introduce good musique, but he never could do it, there never having been any musique here better than ballads...That he hath gathered our Italians from several Courts in Christendome, to come to make a concert for the King, which he do give £200 a year apiece to...And I indeed do commend him for it; for I think it is a very noble undertaking. He do intend to have some times of the year these operas to be performed at the two present theatres, since he is defeated in what he intended in Moorfields on purpose for it. And he tells me plainly that the City audience was as good as the Court; but now they are most gone...Having done our discourse we all took coaches...to Mrs. Knipp's chamber, where this Italian is to teach her to sing her part. And so we all thither, and there she did sing an Italian song or two very fine, while he played the base upon a Harpsicon there; and exceedingly taken I am with her singing, and believe she will do miracles at that and acting'.

In the end Killigrew never managed either to build an opera house in Moorfields or to mount Italian opera seasons at Drury Lane. But it is interesting that the intention was there 50 years before anyone succeeded.

The spirits of Londoners sank still further the following June when the Dutch fleet raided the Thames and Medway ports. Although the government had been warned of the Dutch attack by one of their spies in Holland, the future playwright Aphra Behn, they ignored her intelligence and were caught completely by surprise. The navy's flagship was captured, along with a frigate, and much of the rest of the fleet burnt at its moorings – some ships scuppered on the orders of Monck (now Duke of Albemarle) to prevent further humiliation. A month later Charles ended the war with the Treaty of Breda and sacked his chief minister, Lord Chancellor Clarendon. The government was effectively bankrupt.

Killigrew was not finding much profit at the Theatre Royal either. Dryden took his best comic script yet, *Sir Martin Mar-all*, to D'Avenant at The Duke's. D'Avenant also seemed to be finding the best actors – maybe his training school in Hatton Garden was better than Killigrew's at the Barbican. In early October Pepys managed to get himself invited by Mary Knepp into the dressing room at Drury Lane where he, to his delight, found Nell Gwynne,

'all unready, and is very pretty, prettier than I thought...but to see how Nell cursed for having so few people in the pit was strange; the other house carrying away all the people at the new play and is said now-a-days to have generally most company.'

Perhaps she was wishing she had stayed in Epsom where she had spent the early part of the summer in a short but enjoyable liaison with the Earl of Dorset, the poet and wit, Lionel Buckhurst. D'Avenant's company was clearly in the ascendancy but it was knocked badly when he died on 7 April the following year, 1668. For London theatre it was a great loss for he had been the most energetic and daring impressario for nearly 40 years, as well as a fluent and prolific writer. Thomas Killigrew, his rival for so long, paid tribute to D'Avenant by staging his play *The Man's the Master* at the Theatre Royal exactly a month after his death, with Nell Gwynne in her only role as a boy.

At some time in these months young Henry Purcell, aged about seven or eight, joined the Chapel Royal. The first group of choristers who had been signed up at the Restoration were now leaving as their voices broke. Michael Wise (returning home as the future organist at Salisbury Cathedral: he was killed in 1687 by being hit on the head in an argument with the night watchmen) and Thomas Edwards, who went to work for Pepys, had left in 1664. Pelham Humfrey and John Blow moved on in May 1665, just as the court was retreating from the plague. Humfrey, however, remained in royal service, travelling to France ostensibly to study music in Paris though quite probably to engage in a spot of discreet spying on the king's behalf. Whitehall Palace was said to be rife with Louis XIV's spies. Charles could have done with a few independent sources of his own.

Humfrey returned a year later, with a very high opinion of himself and a very low opinion of his English musical colleagues, to take up an appointment as Musician in Ordinary for the lute.

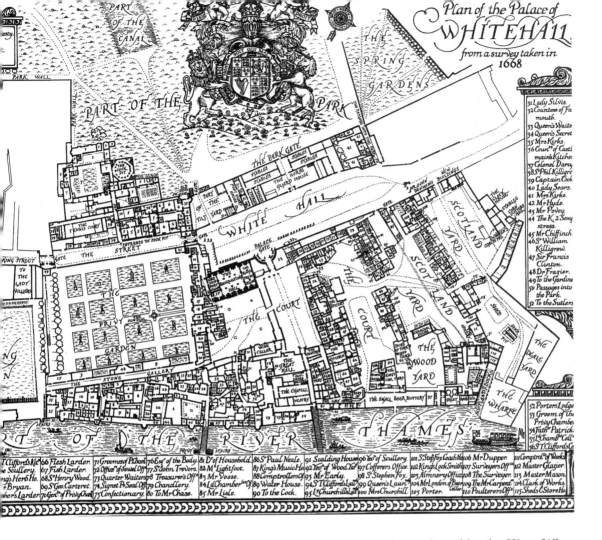

Plan of the Palace of
WHITEHALL
from a survey taken in
1668

PART OF THE CANAL

PART OF THE PARK

PARK WALL

THE SPRING GARDENS

THE PARK GATE

STABLES

THE HORSE GUARD HOUSE

WHITE HALL

THE TILT YARD

THE STREET

THE TENNIS COURT

KING STREET
TO THE LADY VILLIARS

THE PRIVY GARDEN

THE STONE GALLERY

SCOTLAND YARD

THE WOOD YARD

THE COURT

THE GREAT HALL

THE CHAPEL

THE COCK PIT

PART OF THE RIVER THAMES

31 Lady Silvis.
32 Countess of Falmouth.
33 Queen's Waite
34 Queen's Secret
35 Mrs Kirks
36 Court of Castlemain's Kitchen
37 Colonel Darcy
38 Sr Phil Killigre
39 Captain Cook
40 Lady Sears.
41 Mrs Kirke.
42 Mr Hyde.
43 Mr Povey.
44 The K. 2 Sempstress.
45 Mr Chiffinch.
46 Sr William Killigrew.
47 Sir Francis Clinton.
48 Dr Frazier.
49 To the Gardine
50 Passages into the Park.
52 To the Sutlers

52 Porters Lodge
53 Groom of the Privy Chambe
54 Fath Patrick.
51 Chamb Cell
55 Sr Clifford's C

66 Flesh Larder. 67 Fish Larder. 68 Sr Henry Wood. 69 Sr Geo Carteret. 70 Gent of Privy Cha.
71 Groomes of Chan. 72 Office of Sewel Off. 73 Quarter Waiters Off. 74 Signet Pr Seal Off. 75 Confectionary.
76 Esqr of the Body. 77 Sr John Trevors. 78 Treasurers Off. 79 Chandlery. 80 To Mr Chase.
81 Dr of Household. 82 Mr Lightfoot. 83 Mr Yosse. 84 Ld Chamber Of. 85 Mr Lisle.
86 Sr Paul Neale. 87 King's Musick Ho. 88 Comptrollers Of. 89 Water House. 90 To the Cock.
91 Scalding House. 92 Yeo of Wood Yar. 93 Mr Early. 94 Sr Clifford's Lau. 95 Ld Churchill's Lau.
96 Yeo of Scullery. 97 Cofferers Office. 98 Sr Stephen Fox. 99 Queen's Laun. 100 Mrs Churchill.
101 Sr Steph Fox Coach Ho. 102 Kings Lock Smith. 103 Almnery Office. 104 Mr London & Barn. 105 Porter.
106 Mr Dupper. 107 Surveyers Off. 108 The Surveyer. 109 The Mr Carpent. 110 Poulterers Off.
111 Comptrol of Works. 112 Master Glazier. 113 Master Mason. 114 Clark of Works. 115 Sheds & Store Ho.

The ramshackle Palace of Whitehall in 1668, seat of Royal and civil government.
The choristers lodgings were just across the road from the Privy Garden, the Chapel Royal was near the river in the centre of the picture, and the Music House was in the cluster of buildings dividing Scotland Yard from The Court.

It was an opinion that may have been shared by the King. When the much-revered Nicholas Lanier died in February 1666 Charles replaced him as Master of the King's Musick not with John Banister, who as Lanier's deputy might have expected the post, but with the Frenchman Louis Grabu who had arrived in England just before Humfrey left. Humfrey was not too impressed by Grabu either – '[he] understands nothing, nor can play on any instrument, and so cannot compose' was his verdict. It was unfair for, although Grabu was no Lully and was to be put in the shade by Purcell and Blow, his music for the stage later in the reign was good enough to impress Dryden as being better than anyone else's in London and he was an accomplished organist. However Grabu was sacked from his court post in 1674, though by then it was more likely to have been as a result of the new Test Act (which forced all holders of public office to take an oath accepting the rites of the Church of England) than for musical incompetence.

As a boy of the Chapel Royal Henry Purcell would probably have boarded with the Master of the Choristers, Captain Henry Cooke. He occupied extensive buildings at the ends and along the side of the palace tennis court in King Street (now Parliament Street), roughly where the Treasury now stands. The Chapel itself was further up Whitehall on the other side of the road, by Whitehall steps, which led down to the river. To get from one to the other the boys would have passed through the Tudor Holbein Gate that separated King Street from Whitehall, turned immediately right through Palace Gate by the side of the Banqueting House, and crossed a yard (unromantically called The Court) to The Great Hall, on the other side of which stood the Chapel. Rehearsals might have taken place in The Music House, which stood a little farther away in a service courtyard which contained The Spicery, The Pastry and the Duke of York's wood yard. The Music House itself was joined by the Comptroller of the Household's office, the keeper of the King's beer cellar and the house of Sir Paul Neale.

Henry Cooke was in charge of all the living arrangements for the boys and their general education. For their food, lodging, laundry and lessons he was allowed £30 per boy per year (although for Pelham Humfrey, who had been considered a quite exceptional singer, he had been paid £40). He was also responsible for providing them with their uniforms; liveries consisting of scarlet cloaks, lined with velvet for winter and satin for summer, suits the same colour trimmed with silver and shirts with lace cuffs. It sounds smart and would have been had the Treasurer paid Cooke. But by 1667 Cooke was owed nearly £600 in pay and expenses and he sought to prosecute the officer of the wardrobe responsible for payment. The following January he went on strike, refusing to let the boys sing in the Chapel because their clothes were not fit to be seen. Cooke was not the only one to be in arrears. Almost all the musicians, including many who had lost their homes and belongings in the fire, were owed sums dating back to the Restoration. Things did not improve, even though the King and the Lords of the Treasury made the appropriate promises, largely because there was simply no money in the royal purse. A combination of incompetence, extravagance, the war and an insufficient income from taxes to maintain a modern state meant that Charles II was perpetually broke. He had married Catherine of Braganza largely because she came with a dowry of £30,000. He became increasingly reliant on secret grants from Louis XIV and survived largely by surcharging the estates of out-of-favour aristocrats and diverting excise creatively.

Cooke refused to let the choristers out of the house again in 1670, claiming that they were 'unfit to attend his Majesty, or walk in the streets'. Once again promises were made and this time they were partly kept, Cooke being given some of the revenue from the licenses issued to wine merchants, but by the time he died two years later he was owed well over £1,000. He richly deserved to have been paid, given the extraordinary group of musicians that passed through his choir school. Besides the brilliant composers that emerged there were also the remarkable organists, like Michael Wise, Thomas Tudway, John Blow and Henry Hall who went on to rebuild the musical reputations of some of the great churches around the country; Wise to Salisbury Cathedral, Hall to Hereford, Blow to Westminster Abbey and Tudway to King's College, Cambridge.

Cooke, of course, was not teaching alone. Between them the Chapel Royal and Westminster Abbey, physically only a few hundred yards apart, could offer tutors of astonishing quality: Christopher Gibbons (the immensely likeable son of the great Orlando Gibbons) taught the boys organ and other keyboard instruments like the virginals; John Banister taught violin and its older cousins, the viols; John Hingston explained the mechanics of the instruments and Matthew Locke was among those on hand to guide early compositions. There were also lessons on the family of lutes and a good general education for the time, consisting of reading and writing, mathematics, Latin and, given its prevalence at court, probably some French.

The boys were encouraged not only by their masters to compose but by the King, who asked at least once a month and sometimes more to hear the work they produced, often anthems with full instrumental accompaniments, in the chapel services. This was partly a matter of genuine interest on Charles's part, partly too that he found the compositions of the older generation of composers rather dull and preferred the new and livelier baroque style with its elements of French dance music. It is likely that Henry Purcell was one of the children who benefited and there is a tradition that when he was eleven he composed an ode for King Charles's fortieth birthday in June 1670. Pelham Humfrey, by then one of the teachers, is meant to have copied the piece but the manuscript seems to have disappeared sometime in the nineteenth century.

Wren's Dorset Garden Theatre for the Duke's Company built in 1671 at a cost of £9,000. It's name was changed to the Queen's Theatre in 1689 and was the main venue for Purcell's semi-operas. It seems to have fallen out of use in the early years of the 18th century, to be replaced by the Covent Garden Theatre in 1732.

The boys were not confined to Whitehall Palace and the royal trips to Hampton Court and Windsor. They were also encouraged to join the adult members of the Chapel Royal in working for the two chartered theatres which were technically also part of the court's artistic establishment. While the use of women on stage meant that the boys were no longer needed to take the female parts, as they had done earlier in the century, they were still useful for choruses, songs too difficult to be tackled by the actors and of course children's roles. Their participation was needed more often when the Duke's Company, now managed by Betterton and Henry Harris (with D'Avenant's widow Marie de Tremblay running the administration), moved into a new theatre more suited to operatic productions, in 1671. The old tennis court in Lincoln's Inn Fields had been less than satisfactory for a long time and Sir William D'Avenant had begun to plan the move well before his death three years earlier. Wren designed the new building, which was much larger than Drury Lane and cost, at £9,000, six times as much as Killigrew's theatre had a decade earlier. It occupied a magnificent site left vacant by the Great Fire at the junction of the River Fleet and the Thames, a few yards from where the old Salisbury Court Theatre had been.

The Dorset Garden Theatre, as it was named, had a fine neo-classical facade surmounted by the arms of the Duke of York, Prince James, and the audience could arrive by boat at Dorset

Steps – particularly convenient for those wishing to come along from Whitehall. Inside there was seating for 1,200 people facing a magnificently decorated proscenium arch. Its stage machinery represented the greatest technical advance London theatre had seen since the introduction of groove and shutter scenery 50 years before. The theatre opened on 9 November 1671 with a revival of *Sir Martin Mar-all*. John Dryden usually wrote for The King's Company but this play had been something of a coup for D'Avenant, within a week of whose death Dryden had succeeded as Poet Laureate.

Even though Dryden was normally one of his stable of writers, Killigrew was finding it difficult to match Betterton and Harris, with their knack of stirring up interest with authors like Aphra Behn, the first woman to tackle contemporary subjects with an equal wit to Etherege and Sedley. The previous Christmas Killigrew had tried to take the initiative by presenting Dryden's hugely ambitious two-part tragedy *The Conquest of Granada* (to give it its full title, *Almanzor and Almahide, or The Conquest of Granada by the Spaniards)*. His secret weapon had been in casting as Almahide Nell Gwynne, whom he enticed back to the stage after an absence of over a year, during which time she had become the King's latest mistress. Although Charles had met her several years before he does not seem to have taken her as a lover until seeing her in Dryden's *Tyrhannic Love* in the spring of 1669. Nell, aged 20, was soon pregnant, as Dryden made quite clear in the epilogue to his delayed play about Granada.

> 'Think him not duller for the year's delay;
> He was prepared, the women were away:
> And men without their parts can hardly play.
> If they through sickness seldom did appear,
> Pity the virgins of each theatre;
> For at both houses 'twas a sickly year!
> And pity us, your servants, to whose cost
> In one such sickness nine whole months were lost.'

In the event, while *The Conquest of Granada* marked Nell's return, it was also her swan song. She retired a month later, a few days after her twenty-first birthday, when both parts of the play were performed in Whitehall Palace on 10 and 11 February 1671. By then she had left her actress's lodgings in Lincoln's Inn Fields and moved nearer her lover – not into the Palace, where she would have had to jostle with all the other

Nell Gwynne (1650-1687), aged about 22 with her son, the Duke of St. Alban's, painted for Charles II's private delectation by Lely.

mistresses, but into a new and fashionable house at 79, Pall Mall, overlooking St James's Park. She had the good sense to refuse the offered lease and insisted on the freehold, making it the only property on the south side of the street not owned by the Crown, as it still is. Without Nell Gwynne, Killigrew's company was beginning to look lacklustre. Worse was to follow the next year when, on 25 June 1672, a fire at his theatre left it unusable and destroyed the whole scenery and wardrobe stock. He was forced to reopen D'Avenant's shoddy old building in Lincoln's Inn Fields.

Among the musicians the summer of 1672 was one of upheaval as well. Henry Cooke fell seriously ill in June, resigning his position as Marshall of the Corporation of Musick – effectively the official representative of the composers, singers and players. George Hudson, one of the two court composers, was also too ill to carry out his work. Cooke died in the middle of July, Hudson was dead by December. Their various duties were divided between Pelham Humfrey and Thomas Purcell. Humfrey took charge of the Chapel Royal choristers and became Composer in the Private Musick for Voices. Thomas Purcell was made Marshall of the Corporation of Musick. They had been sharing Hudson's work without fee since January and they were both given the title of Composer in Ordinary for the Violins, though they had to wait until August 1673 for the appointment to be confirmed. For the payment of their £52 15/10d, moreover, they had to wait until Michaelmas. Thomas Purcell was also owed £71 11/10d for other wages and livery going back four and three-quarter years. He was beginning to accumulate important jobs and his increasing status was reflected in his new address, in Pall Mall a few houses along from Nell Gwynne.

For most of the previous decade the fashion for private music meetings begun in the Commonwealth had flourished. They were either made up of amateur groups gathering in private houses for a drink (which was charged for) and a song (which was not) – the equivalent of the 18th and 19th century glee clubs: or they were rather more professional (though often not very distinguished) ensembles playing in 'musicke-houses', taverns often with a room set aside for the purpose. Here too the music was free, though the listeners were expected to tip the players. At one stage, in 1656, the puritan Parliament had tried to ban such places but it failed and the music-houses thrived, often using as their basic instrument one of the organs removed on parliamentary orders from the churches.

Just after Christmas 1672 John Banister, who had been passed over for the post of Master of the King's Musique largely because he had failed to pass on fees to his fellow musicians, made the first attempt to promote music for money.

'These are to give notice,' announced the *London Gazette* on 30 December, 'that at Mr. John Banister' House, now called the Musick-school, over against the George Tavern in White Fryers, this present Monday, will be musick performed by Excellent Masters, beginning precisely at four of the clock in the afternoon, and every afternoon for the future, precisely at the same hour.'

John Banister (1625-1679), composer, violinist and teacher, whose public concerts with paid admission were the world's first.

Banister was a famous violin teacher as well as player and it is more than possible that these afternoon events, the world's first public concerts, were as much to show off the skill of his students as to provide more work for his fellow players. With Killigrew's company operating at less than full strength the fifteen or so musicians that usually played for his theatre may have been left with rather too much unpaid time on their hands. Interestingly, unlike modern concert players who relish spotlights and public adulation, performers in the 1670s were hidden from the audience. Roger North, one of the most enthusiastic amateurs of the century whose brother was Lord Keeper of the Great Seal, left two accounts of Banister's concerts which, although written only two years apart, are delightfully contradictory about the quality.

'The first attempt was low: a project of old Banister, who was a good

37

violin and a theatrical composer. He opened an obscure room in a publik house in White fryers; filled it with tables and seats and made a side box with curtains for the musick. 1/- a piece, call for what you please, pay the reckoning, and Welcome gentlemen. Here came most of the shack [rough] performers in towne, and much company to hear; and divers musical curiositys were presented, as for instance, Banister himself upon a flageolett in consort, which was never heard again before nor since unless imitated by the high manner upon the violin.'

Banister's room was just round the corner from North's chambers in the Temple. North seems to have had a rosier memory of the concerts the next time he wrote about them.

'There was very good musick, for Banister found means to procure the best hands in towne, and some voices to come and performe there, and there wanted no variety of humour, for Banister himself (inter alia) did wonders upon a flageolett to a thro-base, and the severall masters had their solos.'

By the summer of 1673 it was clear that it would soon be time for the young Henry Purcell to graduate from among the boys of the Chapel Royal. In those days, when children's general health and diet delayed puberty, fourteen was considered quite an early age for treble voices to break – John Blow, for example, had been nearly sixteen and Pelham Humfrey seventeen. The issue must have arisen of how to train him. There never seems to have been any question of him not going into the family business. Quite apart from Henry's obvious talent, Thomas Purcell's growing influence both as a musician and as a trusted servant of the King made the court the most likely employer for his family. An apprenticeship was one sensible option, especially since living at home was not a problem, either with Elizabeth Purcell in Westminster or Thomas Purcell in St James's.

The solution was to make Henry assistant to the long-serving John Hingston, one of the most respected musical figures of the time who had been as indispensable to Cromwell as he was to Charles II for his knowledge of the practical side of music. Hingston supervised the care of all instruments at court, which meant the various organs in the chapels at Whitehall, Somerset House (the Queen's residence), Hampton Court and Windsor as well as the wind instruments used by the royal orchestra. Stringed instruments seem to have been the responsibility of their players, although Hingston's department was at least partly responsible for supplying them. The warrant issued on Henry's behalf on 10 June 1673 gives all the details:-

'to admit Henry Purcell in the place of keeper, maker, mender, repayrer and tuner of the regalls, organs, virginalls, flutes and recorders and all other kind of wind instruments whatsoever, in ordinary, without fee, to his Majesty, and assistant to John Hingston, and upon the death or other avoydance of the latter, to come in ordinary with fee.'

It is interesting that it was even then accepted that Henry would be Hingston's successor in a position of great responsibility to his fellow musicians and he was soon taking on some of the chores for Hingston, as we know from an order for two violins signed by Purcell the following year. Working as Hingston's deputy was also a wonderful grounding for a composer, giving him an unparallelled understanding of the capabilities of the instruments for which he would be writing. At 14 he would not have been too disturbed by the lack of pay. For one thing the family was comfortable, even if not rich. For another it was quite likely that he would anyway have had to wait years for the exchequer to pay him. He was not left completely without resources, however. At the end of October 1673 he was given an annual grant of £30 – the same amount as Humfrey would have received for keeping Purcell as a chorister – and in December he was given 'the usual clothing' since his voice had changed and he had 'gone from the Chapel'. There was the odd bit of work to be picked up at Westminster Abbey too, though it did not exactly pay a fortune. Over the next few years he was paid £2 for tuning the organ and £5 for copying parts, work that John Blow was no doubt relieved to hand over to his pupil.

Meanwhile there was more musical activity in the theatre than there had been for several years and it is likely that Purcell, accomplished and not over-burdened with court work, would have had some part in it. Betterton does not seem initially to have been as interested in dramatic music as D'Avenant (with all his memories of Paris) had been. Nonetheless through Killigrew's enthusiasm opera in London received a new spur in 1673 with the arrival in London of the Duke of York's second wife, Mary of Modena (his first, Clarendon's daughter Anne Hyde, had died two years before).

Marrying Mary, at first by proxy, was an act of defiance on James's part. He had just been forced to resign his post as First Lord of the Admiralty by Parliament which, in order to destroy Charles's attempts at introducing religious toleration – ironically one of the things the old Parliament had insisted on in the Declaration of Breda at the Restoration – had pushed through the Test Act which debarred Catholics and other dissenters from public office. Since by then James's Catholicism was public, having his marriage arranged via the French court (which promised a dowry of 400,000 crowns as an incentive) was deliberately provocative. Parliament, in fact, expressly forbade it but too late; by then James had ensured that he was married.

Mary of Modena (1658-1718) who married James, Duke of York (the future James II) in 1673 when she was 15.

Mary of Modena arrived in London in November 1673. A few weeks before, another import from the French court had also settled there. This was Robert Cambert, the father-figure of French opera who had found himself unable to work at home thanks to Lully's success in securing a monopoly on opera production in Paris. His pupil Louis Grabu was Master of the King's Musick in London and Cambert no doubt thought he would have better luck there. Charles and James were well known for their partiality to French music and the King was

Matthew Locke (1622-1677) the father of English music theatre.

keen to show the world that, whatever the actions of his legislature, his court was cosmopolitan and open to continental fashion. He had, after all, just ennobled his latest mistress, Louise de Queroualle – a lady in waiting to his sister, the Duchess of Orleans – by giving her the wonderfully irrelevant title of Duchess of Portsmouth. She was for years to come the go-between for Charles and Louis XIV and had even drawn up the list of eligible French women for James to marry.

Killigrew meanwhile had, like D'Avenant before him, looked to Sir Christopher Wren to provide him with an up-to-date theatre to replace his burnt-out one. It was ready for opening on 26 March 1674. Four nights later it hosted the first of many London institutions over the last four hundred years to be entitled the Royal Academy of Music. This was the nearest Killigrew came to his dream of establishing a separate opera company. This grandiose new Academy represented Grabu and Cambert's attempt to transfer the form of French opera to England. For the occasion they adapted Cambert's *Ariane*, originally composed in 1661 and rehearsed, but never publicly performed, in Paris. We do not know who the performers were, or even in which language *Ariane* was sung (the libretto was published in both English and French) but costs were kept down through Grabu borrowing scenery from the court theatre at Whitehall Palace for a fortnight.

As usual though, Betterton's instinct had pre-empted Killigrew. For many years the Duke's Company had been reviving a semi-operatic version of *Macbeth* with music by Matthew Locke. In the autumn of 1673 Betterton turned to Locke again to produce something to appeal to the rising taste for all things French. For a libretto he turned to Thomas Shadwell who had just scored a hit with his comedy *Epsom Wells*. Shadwell soon came up with a version of Moliere's *Psyche* (which he claimed to have improved) and quickly learned the essentials of libretto writing.

'In all the words which are sung I did not so much take the care of the Wit or Fancy of 'em, as the making of 'em proper for Musick; in which I cannot but have some little knowledge, having been bred, for many years of my youth, to some performance in it. I chalk'd out the way to the Composer...having design'd which Line I wou'd have sung by One, which by Two, which by Three, which by Four Voices &c. and what manner of Humour I would have in all the Vocal Musick...By his excellent Composition, that long known, able and approved Master of Musick, Mr. Lock...has done me a great deal of right; though I believe, the unskilful in Musick, will not like the more solemn part of it...for those who are not so, there are light and airy things to please them.'

The 'light and airy things' were the dances and instrumental tunes which Locke entrusted to his colleague in the Queen's chapel, Giovanni Draghi. Locke published the part that he wrote but not Draghi's, which has not survived. *Psyche* was successful enough for the rival company at the Theatre Royal (still in its temporary home in the old Lincoln's Inn Fields theatre) to produce a parody of it, *Psyche Debauch'd*, by Thomas Duffet a few months later. Locke, famous for his short temper, was not amused.

Betterton was encouraged enough by the success of *Psyche* – which had been an immense investment, with £800 being spent on the scenery by Wren (continuing the tradition set by Inigo Jones of the King's Surveyor also being the principal theatre designer) – to commission the successful team of Locke, Draghi and Shadwell to attempt an even more spectacular opera competing head on with the Cambert and Grabu *Ariane* in April and May 1674. Shadwell, presumably working in an even greater rush than usual, decided to make a third-hand version of *The Tempest*, using Dryden and D'Avenant's rewrite of seven years earlier as the basis. Although the result has been largely responsible for Shadwell's tarnished reputation in later centuries, at the time it was an immense hit, making Betterton even more money than *Psyche*.

No expense was spared on the production, which used the

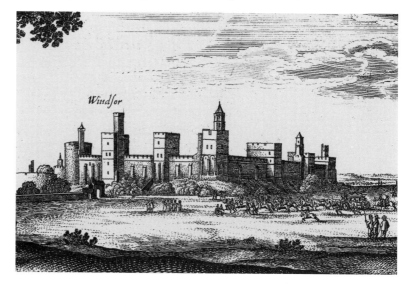

Windsor Castle, where the court spent the early part of each summer, drawn in the middle of the 17th century by Wenceslas Hollar.

42

full '24 violins' of the court orchestra – double the normal theatre size. Normally at that time of year the court left London for Windsor, so providing performers for the theatre and the chapel was a logistical nightmare, as the royal warrant for the arrangements makes clear.

'It is his Majesties pleasure that Mr. Turner & Mr. Hart, or any other men or Boyes belonging to his Majestys Chapell Royall that sing in ye *Tempest* at His Royal Highnesse Theatre doe remain in Towne all the weeke during his Majestys absence from Whitehall to perform that service, Only Saterdayes to repair to Windsor and to returne to London on Mundayes if there be occasion for them.'

Locke and Draghi wrote the extensive instrumental music between them (Locke's is some of his most evocative writing) but the vocal numbers set by John Banister for the 1667 production – including a lovely version of 'Full Fathom Five' – were retained. Shadwell's own music teacher, Pietro Reggio, contributed one song but the main operatic contents were the two masques inserted by Shadwell and elegantly set by Pelham Humfrey. It was the most elaborate staging seen in London since the Restoration and its splendour can be imagined from the description printed at the beginning of Shadwell's text.

'The Front of the Stage is open'd, and the Band of 24 Violins, with the harpsicals and Theorbo's which accompany the Voices, are plac'd between the pit and the Stage. While the Overture is playing, the Curtain rises, and discovers a new Frontispiece, joined to the great Pilasters on each side of the stage. This Frontispiece is a noble Arch, supported by large wreathed Columns of the Corinthian Order; the wreathing of the Columns are beautifi'd with Roses wound about them, and several Cupids flying about them. On the Cornice, just over the Capitals, sits on either side a Figure, with a trumpet in one hand, and a Palm in the other, representing Fame...Behind this is the Scene, which represents a thick Cloudy Sky, a very Rocky Coast, and a Tempestuous Sea in perpetual Agitation. This Tempest (suppos'd to be rais'd by Magick) has many dreadful objects in it, as several Spirits in horrid shapes flying down amidst the Sailers, then rising and crossing in the Air. And when the Ship is sinking, the whole house is darken'd, and a shower of Fire falls upon them. This is accompanied by Lightning and several Claps of Thunder to the end of the Storm.'

Taking 24 musicians back and forth to Windsor was not cheap. The group – which included Banister, Locke, Humfrey, Nicholas Staggins and Thomas Purcell – cost the exchequer nearly £1,500, with Pelham Humfrey, John Banister and Thomas Purcell receiving well above average fees of £100 each.

For Humfrey *The Tempest* proved to be a final triumph and the journey to Windsor his last, for he died there on 14 July, aged only 27. It was a tragic waste of a talent that all his contemporaries recognised as well out of the ordinary. One wonders whether he would have been well enough three days before to attend or play in a last performance of the French music he so much admired when Cambert's opera *Pomone* – first played in Paris three years before – was given for the King. The same day Cambert and his pupil, the Master of the King's Music, Louis Grabu provided a *Ballet et Musique pour le Divertissement du Roy de la Grande-Bretagne.*

Later that month John Blow was named as Humfrey's

John Blow (1649-1708), Purcell's teacher and closest musical colleague, in a portrait by John Riley.

successor to the posts of Master of the Children of the Chapel Royal and Composer in Ordinary for the Voices. He was of more robust constitution than his childhood friend and held the titles until 1708, providing an invaluable period of continuity which produced, like Cooke's, another generation of brilliant composers and singers. For Blow 1674 was a good summer, for within a few weeks he had married Elizabeth Braddock, the daughter of his colleague Edward at Westminster Abbey.

It was a less happy summer for Grabu and Cambert, for although *Ariane* had been tolerably well received, there was to be no London performance of *Pomone*. Grabu fell foul of the prevailing persecution of Catholics, being relieved of his position as Master of the King's Musick. Thereafter Cambert was out of favour too. It was an ignominious end to the career of a fine composer; excluded from Paris by the manic insecurity of Lully and ignored in London because of religious chauvinism. Grabu's job went to the uninteresting but competent Nicholas Staggins. In 1676 Charles sent him off to the continent to learn to be a little less parochial, appointing Matthew Locke to take his place while he was away.

Locke did not enjoy the privilege for long for in August 1677, at the age of 56, he too died suddenly. It was a great loss for English music for he had been the most colourful and perhaps the most inspired composer of his generation; one who could be held up to his French and Italian contemporaries with pride. This was keenly realised by his 18-year-old pupil, one of whose first published songs was an ode 'On the Death of his Worthy Friend'.

'What hope for us remains now he is gone?
He that knew all the pow'r of Numbers flow'n;
Alas! too soon; Ev'n he, whose skillful Harmony
Had Charms for all the Ills that we Indure,
And could apply a certain cure...'

The answer to the author's question was the composer; Henry Purcell.

Chapter 3

Rise my Love, my Fair One

The appointment of Henry Purcell to Locke's position of Composer in Ordinary for the Violins on 10 September 1677 was an extraordinary one and must have seemed so to his contemporaries. Apart from anything else it must have rankled with some that both orchestral composers' positions were now in the hands of Purcells. Thomas's posts added up to a considerable slice of the musical establishment. Aside from his composership and his non-musical appointment as Groom of the Robes, by this time he was also a Musician in Ordinary, Musician for the Lute and Voices and a Gentleman of the Chapel Royal. In his capacity as Marshal of the Westminster Corporation of Musick he was not only effectively the union representative, he was in charge of making sure that the playing fees were distributed properly. For his young relation – son or nephew – to be promoted at the age of 18, younger even than Pelham Humfrey had been (without the benefit of Humfrey's Parisian training) could have seemed too much of a good thing. Odder still was the fact than neither Purcell was at that time known for his violin compositions. Thomas, it seems, never was. We have almost none of his music now (unless some has been misattributed – and it is possible that his manuscripts could have been burnt in the 1698 fire that destroyed Whitehall Palace, as Nicholas Staggins's were). Nonetheless it is peculiar, if he was as active as his roster of appointments suggests, that we have so few references to him or his music.

Whitehall Palace in about 1650. On the left is the Banqueting House (still standing), straight ahead is the Holbein Gate.

The duties of the Composer for the Violins were varied. He was expected to produce and prepare music for the day to day life of the court: music for dancing, mealtimes (whether the king was eating semi-privately or in a formal banquet), state entertainments and for accompanying the choir in the Chapel Royal. The last duty involved making sure that the group of players drawn from the full band actually turned up and rehearsed – given the government's habit of paying late it is not surprising that they preferred outside engagements when they could get them. The violins also played at the two patent theatres, half the band being assigned to each. By 1677, of course, the orchestra had a good stock of what we would now call light music – by Staggins, Locke, Grabu, Draghi, Banister and many others – foreign as well as home-grown. They did not, however, have much by Purcell, Thomas or either Henry, senior or junior. For the latter to have been given one of the half-dozen most important musical jobs in the country, even considering Charles's tendency to act on whim, there must have been some evidence that he was capable of fulfilling it. The recommendation could have come from Thomas, or from Matthew Locke himself before he died. It is most likely, however, that his main champion was John Blow, who from evidence later in their lives, took great pride in his part in Purcell's education. Blow would have seen the early anthems and songs that the young composer was producing. He would have appreciated their potential and no doubt applauded the diligence with which Purcell copied out and studied the works of older composers.

For the two years after Purcell was given the composer's post in the autumn of 1677 we have surprisingly little information about his activities. There are a few anthems which are usually dated to this time – like *My Beloved Spake*, reckoned to be his first anthem that needed the full chapel complement of choir and strings – but otherwise it seems likely that although he held the appointment he was in reality still pursuing his studies with Blow and assisting Hingston with the care of instruments. Although delays at the exchequer were by this time more common than not, it may be significant that payment of his salary and livery grant was not authorised until December 1679.

There has been a suggestion that in 1678 he enrolled as a student at Westminster School. Even allowing for 17th-century attendance ages, which were more elastic than they are today,

Westminster School in the early 19th century. It had changed little since the 17th century except for the building of the classical arch up to the main school hall which rises above the Tudor houses of the masters.

it seems extremely unlikely that he would have re-entered formal schooling at nearly nineteen. There is no tradition at the school of Purcell having been a boy there and as an institution it is rarely slow to claim great alumni. Dr. Richard Busby, the headmaster for 50 years, certainly knew Purcell but later, as an Abbey official. Dryden and his son were both there and, had he and Purcell attended the same school, one might have thought that Dryden would have referred to it somewhere. There was a Henry Purcell in the school as a Bishop's scholar but not until well after his namesake's appointment as Abbey organist. There was also a Charles Purcell, who may have been the composer's brother or cousin but he left at the age of 15, making it even more unlikely that it was the composer who suddenly decided on a strict regime of Latin and rhetoric at four years older.

Henry Purcell began to emerge into the public gaze in 1679. John Playford, the most important music publisher in London, issued five of his songs in the second book of *Choice Ayres and Songs*. These may have been Purcell's first works in print and it was an impressive beginning. There was the *Elegy* for Matthew Locke (a setting of an ode by Abraham Cowley) and some lighter songs; *Scarce had the Rising Sun Appear'd, Amintas, To My Grief I See, Since the Pox,* and *I Resolve Against Cringing.*

48

While Purcell may have still been learning his trade he was already an accomplished composer who knew how to please his contemporaries, not least the King. It is worth taking a few moments to look in detail at his first important anthem, *My Beloved Spake,* because it shows all the elements that were forming Purcell's characteristic style – and it can still be heard regularly in English Cathedrals. Purcell was a child of the court and his tastes and attitudes were shaped by those who lived and worked in the few streets of Westminster and the Palace of Whitehall. On the rare occasions that he had left the area when he was young it was only to travel with the same group of people a little farther up the Thames – to Hampton Court or Windsor. Unlike Humfrey or Staggins he never travelled farther afield to soak up the atmosphere of other European centres. Despite the fact that London was by far the biggest city in Britain and Purcell was brought up in the very heart of it, there was something of the village about Charles II's court. Half a mile's walk in any direction from the Chapel Royal of the time would cover all the places of importance in Purcell's life with the exception of the Dorset Garden Theatre, which was all of a mile away.

Despite this, Charles II's own experience in his twenties on the continent made him the most outward looking monarch in 100 years. Whatever his foreign policy – fashioned as much by the prejudices of Parliament as by his own inclination – Charles was in continual awe of his cousin Louis in France and the splendour of Catholic courts in Italy. Protestantism was a political necessity but it was temperamentally alien to him. Protestants were, in his mind, either dull and vindictive – like the Bishops of his time – or potentially revolutionary. They had, after all, killed his father, banished him and his mother and were in a state of almost continual rebellion in Scotland. Charles, like his eventual successor William of Orange, personally could not care less what people believed as long as their beliefs did not interfere with the workings of the state. The fact that religious factionalism increasingly dominated his reign was a matter of some disgust to him.

When Charles went to his Chapel, therefore, he wanted a service that he could enjoy in the best spirit of Christian humanism. Enjoyment was central to it. He was lucky enough to have around him one of the finest group of musicians that England has ever produced and they were there to be used. However this did not mean that he wished to have to sit

Whitehall Palace from the Thames. On the left are the King's apartments, with the Queen's in the centre and the roof of the Chapel Royal to the right.

through music of academic turgidity. Unlike many of his subjects, he saw no reason why the church should not be a place of fashion and of ornate beauty. He was a truly baroque King, expecting his artists (and perhaps his mistresses) to embellish nature without losing its form; to engage the passion in as direct a way as possible while exhibiting the most ingenious artistry. He liked intellectual simplicity allied to grace and imagination. His temperament was more like that of his Grandfather, James VI of Scotland (James I of England) who thought carefully enough about the nature of royal authority to have written a treatise on it, but who enjoyed the ribald humour and gorgeous scenery of Shakespeare and Jonson's writing and Jones's designs much more than the world of complicated allegory preferred by the more insecure Charles I and James II. It was an age when a sense of humour, proportion and flexibility were qualities more likely to keep the troublesome thrones of England, Scotland and Ireland intact than was an inflated view of the connection between royalty and divinity. Charles II clearly enjoyed allegorical references comparing him to Caesar, Albion and the rest but from him they seem to have elicited an appreciative smile rather than pompous self-aggrandisement.

These too are the humours which Purcell plays with in *My Beloved Spake*. King Charles found organ accompaniments tedious, so on Sundays when he attended the full service in the Chapel Royal he expected to hear a new anthem with strings supporting the voices. He was not particularly keen on trumpets and wind instruments – unlike William of Orange, (interestingly Purcell barely used them until William's reign.) Charles II also expected to be able to listen to music that set his foot tapping and so the rhythms of French courtly dances underpinned the solid liturgy of the church of England. He had an absolute loathing of the fancy, the English chamber music form which had been the main medium for the consort of viols in his father and grandfather's time. The fancy is not a dance form. It is nearer to the language that a 150 years later would come to characterise the string quartet. This detestation on the part of the King meant that the older composers (like Henry Lawes and William Child) were made to sound a little old fashioned and provincial compared to those who were prepared to adopt the jauntier, more cosmopolitan styles favoured by the royal family. It helps to explain the appointment of men like Louis Grabu and Giovanni Draghi. They may not have been very good continental composers but to the King their music had the virtue that it did not taste of music that Cromwell had liked, even if regulars among the Chapel Royal congregation found the music that the younger composers produced frivolous.

The anthem was a form in which the composer could choose and manipulate the text. For the composers of the Chapel Royal it was also a showpiece as much for instrumental and vocal ingenuity as for religious meaning. Charles liked to hear the words clearly. He did not want the meaning lost in a wash of contrapuntal virtuosity – in this too he showed he was a man of his baroque time, rejecting the polyphonic showmanship of the Elizabethan mannerist age and men like Thomas Tallis. Verse anthems, in which the choir was subordinate to a few solo voices, interwoven with instrumental interludes (always referred to as symphonies, even when they were only a few bars long) were therefore more likely to find favour. Political points in the text were acceptable – although the King was not fond of being preached at by clerics, poets or composers.

Charles II in the 1680s.

All of this must have been at the forefront of the teenage Purcell's mind as he set to work on his first major composition in his new post. *My Beloved Spake* is a daring display. In twelve minutes of music Purcell sets out the elements that are to define his style for the rest of his life: brilliant word setting, infectious rhythms, melodies that seem simple and inevitable – yet are full of complex harmony – opportunities for the best singers on hand to shine and instrumental writing that perfectly sets the mood. The text is taken, not from a stern part of the Bible, but from the Song of Solomon. It is as near to being a secular text as he was likely to get away with in the chapel. The King, who had a good handful of mistresses lodging in the Palace at the time, would have appreciated the invocation 'Rise my love, my fair one, and come away.' But it is less cynical than that.

Purcell divides the four verses of the biblical words into eight verses for soloists and two choruses, with seven instrumental 'symphonies' After an opening dance the title words are tossed around between solo alto, tenor and two basses. Then Purcell combines the lover's passion with the joy of the changing seasons, contrasting music of almost Dowland-like melancholy for 'Lo the winter is past, the rain is over and gone' with thoroughly modern bright writing for the 'flowers appear on the earth; the time of the singing of birds is come.' This becomes steadily more cheerful, ending in a thoroughly non-biblical 'hallelujah.' Then in his most daring stroke he produces harmony of extraordinary voluptuousness when 'the voice of the turtle is heard in our land', a mood which is recaptured in the sheer longing of 'Rise my love, my fair one, and come away.' After this Purcell skips a couple of verses so that he can provide a happy ending: 'my beloved is mine, and I am his; Hallelujah.' He would go on to write longer and more spectacular works in the course of his royal duties but the assurance of this anthem from a composer not yet 20 must have justified the faith of those who had put him forward so untested for Matthew Locke's old job the previous autumn.

1679 was a difficult year for the court and therefore unsettling for the Purcell family. With Thomas and Henry royal composers, Henry's younger brother Daniel just starting as a chorister at the Chapel Royal and his elder brother Edward a Gentleman Usher their prosperity was entirely dependent on the never very efficient working of the Lord Steward's department. The idiocy of the Popish Plot invented by Titus Oates had brought the country as near to the reopening of a civil war as it had been since the days before Charles's restoration. Governments came and went with the seasons. Lord Danby, who had been responsible for putting the state finances under some sort of control, found himself impeached and sent to the Tower of London (by now a rather more gentlemanly place of confinement than it had been in Henry VIII's day). Charles appointed the main opposition leaders as his ministers, with the Earl of Shaftesbury as Lord President of the Council. He had no sympathy for their views, which centred on the exclusion of the Duke of York from the throne as a Catholic and the advancement of Charles's oldest illegitimate son, the Duke of Monmouth, as Protestant heir. But he adopted the principle that he was more likely to be able to divide them against each other when they were nominally in power than when the were out of it. Parliament, even less to Charles's liking than his ministers, was dissolved twice.

Anthony Ashley-Cooper
(1621-1683), Earl of
Shaftesbury, the founder
of the Whig Party.

In the first election of the year, in February, the opposition
won what would now be described as a landslide, with Charles's
supporters occupying only 10 per cent of the seats. It was a
Parliament that knew what it was against but not what it was
for, no more under the control of Shaftesbury than it was of the
King. In the summer it too was dissolved and fresh elections
called. Then in August a bout of flu for Charles turned into
pneumonia and he nearly died. This galvanised his supporters.
James, who had sensibly been told to make himself scarce in
Brussels for most of the year, returned to court. While Charles
was recovering James's influence was decisive. Shaftesbury
found himself out of government once again and Parliament
was first prorogued until December and then told that the King
would not meet it for another year – by which time Charles
calculated (rightly) that the fire would have gone out of it. In
this, if in nothing else, he and Shaftesbury were in agreement.

Charles therefore reverted to his usual policy of enlightened inaction while Shaftesbury rallied electors to sign petitions demanding the meeting of Parliament. Meanwhile James, who to his cost and unlike his brother, always saw issues as either black or white, insisted that people openly declare whether they were for or against him.

In this polarisation of opinion lie the seeds of Britain's two main political parties. The cumbersome labels of 'country' or 'petitioner' and 'abhorrer' (those who abhorred the petitions) were soon abandoned in favour of the terms of abuse hurled by the opposite party. Shaftesbury's followers were identified with puritan Scots republicans (whom both James and his main enemy Monmouth had been trying to control with great brutality) and referred to by the Scots term Whig, slang for a horse thief. In return the King's supporters were called Tories, after the Catholic outlaws who launched raids from Tory Island, a bleak strip of land a few miles off the County Donegal coast of Ireland. For the Whigs, a Tory was the embodiment of self-interest and duplicity, 'a monster with an English face, a French heart and an Irish conscience'. For the Tory, a Whig's language was 'overturn overturn...He prays for the King but with more distinctions and mental reservations than an honest man would have in taking the covenant.' Since taking the covenant was a capital offence in Scotland, it was a serious charge. The Tories are still Tories (in Canada and Britain) and if the Whigs are now Liberals constitutional reform is still their dominant policy.

Purcell and his family were by necessity supporters of the King, though over the coming years it would prove impossible to identify with Protestantism, James II and William III with equal enthusiasm, and no royal servants would find themselves unaffected by the turmoil around them. For Purcell any extra source of money would have been welcome, especially one that had a chance of being paid on time. He took up teaching, sometimes privately, sometimes at the girls schools which had begun to flourish during the Commonwealth years. That owned and managed by Josias Priest – the dancing master and choreographer at the Theatre Royal – and his wife was particularly fashionable and had premises first of all in Leicester Fields and later, when the area became too built up, in Chelsea.

A little extra insurance was provided, along with the dignity of the post, when Purcell took over from Blow as Organist of

Westminster Abbey. The pay was not munificent – £10 a year plus £8 housing allowance – but the Abbey was a more reliable paymaster than the royal household. Blow seems to have relinquished the position voluntarily, pleading pressure of work; not surprisingly considering that he was also Master of the Children of the Chapel Royal and organist there. His administrative duties were leaving him with little time to compose and his duties at Westminster made it difficult for him to supervise the Chapel Royal when it travelled with the King, whether to Windsor, Hampton Court or Newmarket. Blow was also working with the Master of the King's Musick, Staggins, in yet another attempt to form a separate opera company for London. It was a perennial and unrealised ambition throughout the last 70 years of the century, from D'Avenant's ill-timed venture in 1630, to Killigrew and Draghi's (quoted above) and Grabu's 'Royal Academy'. None of them succeeded but each attempt produced a work or two which paved the way for Purcell and Handel.

The Westminster Abbey accounts showing Purcell's salary as Organist of £10 a year.

During the year music outside the court had been hit by the death of John Banister. He had continued his series of concerts every winter for seven years, though the concert rooms had changed and so had the starting times. Banister, whatever his faults as orchestral leader, was a fine composer and set in train the course of events which meant that a 100 years later London was the only capital city in Europe where the public concert, rather than the aristocratic soirée, was at the heart of musical life. His place as an impresario was taken by the most unlikely of men. Thomas Britton was a 'small-coal man', a coal merchant who sold from the sack on his shoulder and had premises in Jerusalem Passage, Clerkenwell Green – close to some of London's most frequented whorehouses. Britton, however, was a man of considerable learning. He had a good library for the time and collected old music and instruments. For 36 years after 1678 he ran concerts every Thursday in a room above his store. They were free – although some regulars may have contributed by subscription – and they were open to everybody. Even more than the theatre, Britton's concerts had no class distinctions. He managed to attract all the best players of the day and it is more than possible, since we know that Handel performed there when he came to London, that Purcell – known to the public as much as a keyboard player as a composer – would also have taken part.

Despite Thomas Britton's initiative it is clear that Banister's more frequent concerts were missed, for the year after his death the world's first purpose-built public concert hall was opened in York Buildings, Villiers Street. The site of the Consort-room, as it was called, was at the bottom of the street, on the east side – close to where Embankment Gardens' bandstand is now. For the Chapel musicians it was extremely convenient, being only a few yards from Whitehall palace itself, and it soon became the place where music previously presented in private to the court could be given to a wider public. Although, if Roger North is to be believed, early events there were often somewhat badly organised, with musicians jostling to take their turn on stage and 'a gabble and bustle while they changed places', the experiment was a success and York Buildings became a feature of London life for the next 50 years. It was also the favoured venue for visiting stars, especially from Italy. Although we do not know how many people the room held, we do know that it was a civilised environment for music with a fine ceiling painted by Antonio Verrio, the Neapolitan artist who was a few years later to succeed Sir Peter Lely as the King's Painter.

For Purcell, the opening of new outlets for his music could not have come at a better time. With Parliament not sitting and the political atmosphere in London thoroughly unpleasant, as far as King Charles was concerned, the King spent as much of his time away from the city as possible – leaving for Windsor in April 1680 and not returning until September. For Purcell, now tied to Westminster Abbey and therefore not part of the group that travelled with the King, the diminution of work at court gave him a wonderful opportunity to compose in peace. He took it with gusto.

Thomas Britton (1644-1714), coal merchant and bibliophile, whose concerts in a room above his office in Aylesbury Street, Clerkenwell (lit by a window 'no bigger than the bung-hole of a cask'), ran from 1678 until his death.

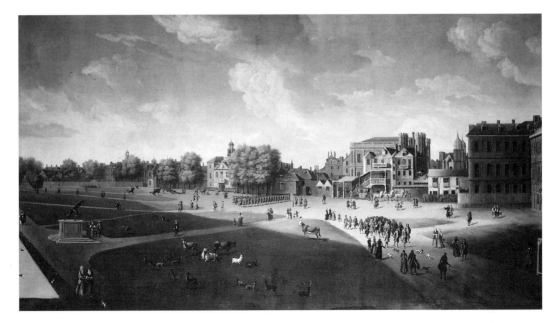

Charles II on Horseguards Parade, 1680. On the left is the St. James's Park canal which predated the present lake.

During the summer of 1680 he worked on music which would not have been primarily for the court. He composed over a dozen chamber works for strings; five *Pavans* for violins and continuo, two In *Nomines* for consort of viols and nine (possibly more) four-part *Fantazias* – seven of them being written in under three weeks. The *Fantazias* in particular are likely to have been for use outside the court, given the King's dislike of the old English fancy, to which these are strongly related. They could have been intended for private music parties but equally they could have been for London's public concerts. Purcell was already established at court and in his musical circle. The songs now appearing in Playford's publications and small-scale works inexpensive to play in public would have been useful in spreading Purcell's name to a wider audience.

Significantly for the future 1680 was also the year that Purcell emerged as a theatre composer. He was engaged to produce the music for the tragedy *Theodosius* or *The Force of Love* by the eccentric (and eventually tragically mad) Nathaniel Lee. Much of the instrumental music and the choruses for performance during the action have not survived – apart from the substantial opening scene. What we do have are the songs written to be heard between the acts, including two of his best known early pieces, *Hail to the Myrtle Shade* and *Ah Cruel Bloody Fate*. The settings are simple and direct, in contrast to Lee's extravagant emotional language, with only recorders and continuo accompanying the voices. Such restraint in the music must have helped to make the play less sentimental and so more poignant for the contemporary audience. That the songs were deemed an important part of the considerable success of *Theodosius* is shown by the fact that, unusually, they were published as an appendix to the printed text. They are extraordinary first ventures and above all they demonstrate Purcell's flexibility, his instinctive gift for suiting his subject matter without compromising his own musical character.

By now Purcell was fulfilling all his obligations as a royal composer, including the requirement to produce at least one valedictory work in praise of the monarch each year. These were expected for New Year, royal birthdays and to welcome the King back to London each autumn. While the actual words of many of these, especially the Welcome Songs (given the awkwardness of political realities) were often little more than fatuous flattery, their intention was serious. On one level they were the inflated equivalent of the twentieth-century habit of playing *God Save the Queen* or – in the case of American Presidents – *Hail to the Chief.* On another these impressive choral cantatas were meant to lift the sovereign above the governmental pressures of the day and mark the effective start of the London political season, just as there is still considerable ceremony (sadly not musical these days) each November when the Queen opens Parliament. For Charles they were meant, as much as anything no doubt, to cheer him up. Being King was something he enjoyed. Being head of a factious and inadequately funded administration was not. Purcell's first attempt at the genre was not, it has to be admitted, one of his best. Yet *Welcome, Vicegerent of the Mighty King* is still more fluent than many of the efforts Charles had to sit through. Even with this first ode Purcell rises above the routine. Like Elgar two hundred years later, Purcell was one of the few English composers who could produce music of high enough quality to be more uplifting than the mundane state occasions for which they were commissioned.

In the case of *Welcome, Vicegerent* it must have been uncomfortably obvious to the audience that the winter's storm of Charles's absence was going to be nothing to the rough ride Parliament was planning for him a few weeks later. So nervous were the authorities that the second play to which Purcell contributed music, Nahum Tate's rewrite of Shakespeare's *Richard II* – with its uncomfortable theme of regicide – was banned. Tate with reluctance reset the material as *The Sicilian*

Usurper, though even he complained that the politically acceptable result was 'obscure and incoherent'. In those days, however, there was no real freedom of artistic expression, even in a court as easy-going as Charles II's. The two theatres, as part of the Royal Household, were in theory attached to the Lord Chamberlain's department and therefore subject to the same official sanction as any other office of state. The alternative (at a time when printing was as closely regulated as broadcasting is now) was to go beyond the law, into the world of unlicensed pamphlets and performances; a risk that carried with it unpleasant penalties. This does not mean that political comment was outlawed, even in the works presented directly at court. The King appreciated words which were applicable to his situation and unlike his father did not expect composers choosing texts or writers to pretend that everything in the land was in a state of perfect harmony, whatever the absurdity of the result. He did expect, however, that those writing while on his payroll should be generally on his side.

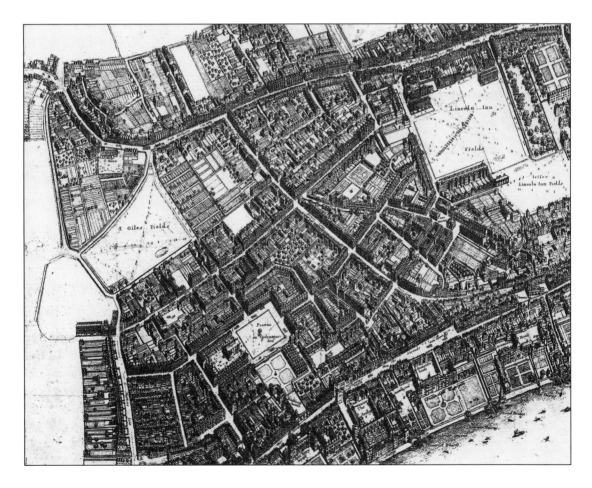

The West End in the 17th century. D'Avenant's converted tennis court theatre sticks out into Lincoln's Inn Fields and the buildings are separated by the formal gardens of the great houses.

In 1680 Purcell was a young man about town in a city that was gaining in confidence and wealth. Much of it was modern, not only because of the new buildings necessitated by the Great Fire 14 years before, but also because of the way landowners were developing their estates. Instead of maintaining large parks around their homes close to the seat of government, those aristocrats lucky enough to own land in the mile between the cities of Westminster and London realised that there was an immense amount of money to be made from urban rents, enough to re-establish the family fortunes diminished in the Civil War. The Earls of Bedford, Leicester, Exeter, Southampton, Salisbury and St.Albans (Henry Jermyn of Jermyn Street), together with Lord Craven, laid out the streets that we now think of as the West End and Covent Garden. In Purcell's time their great houses with fine formal gardens were still there among the tenements, giving the new London the same combination of commercial activity and private grandeur that one finds in Italian cities. Indeed the Bedford estate was modelled directly on Italian experience, with its centrepiece of Inigo Jones's Covent Garden Piazza bounded on the west side by St Paul's Church and on the South by the wall of the splendid Tudor Bedford House, complete with orchard, which was demolished a decade after Purcell's death to make way for more profitable buildings. Some of the lands being developed were hereditary but others, like the Earl of Leicester's (hence Leicester Square) were leased from the Crown.

Henry Purcell in his twenties. The artist is unidentified.

In these new streets developed the Coffee Houses – the first had actually been opened in the City by an enterprising Greek in 1652. By 1680 they had become the most vital part of urban political life. Newsletters were prepared for patrons and different coffee houses began to be associated with different groups and professions. Whigs met at the St James's, Tories at The Cocoa Tree. City merchants involved in imports and therefore shipping met at Lloyd's in Lombard Street. The government was sufficiently worried about the open gatherings and the printing of unlicensed news-sheets that it tried to ban the coffee houses in 1676. The attempt was an abject failure, though, and the worst fears of the authorities were soon realised as the independence of the coffee houses led to alternative postal services, publishing houses and soon daily newspapers.

As well as the Coffee Houses there were taverns of every sort, ranging from drinking dens and whorehouses like the Six Windmills in Chiswell Street, via coaching inns with rooms for travellers to the more respectable sort of eating houses (restaurants as such did not appear for another century or so) – some, as mentioned above, with music rooms. Purcell, like any other gallant young court gentleman without clerical restraints or puritan inhibitions, would have enjoyed London's nightlife. Apart from his theatre music, he was one of the best writers of popular songs of his age, ranging from drinking songs to catches, the words of which shocked the Victorian scholars who rediscovered them and which still appear in the gentrified versions deemed by present-day musicians to be suitable for the modern concert hall. This is of course a totally ridiculous setting for them. They should be enjoyed and joined in with a pint or several of beer late at night in a convivial pub. There is no point in being precious about songs with titles like *As Roger Last Night to Jenny Lay Close* and *The Miller's Daughter Riding* or *Once, Twice, Thrice I Julia Tried* and *Once In Our Lives Let Us Drink To Our Wives*.

After playing his music in York Buildings or going to Dorset Gardens to see *Theodosius* Purcell would have wanted to celebrate. He could have wandered across the Fleet from the theatre into Thames Street and along towards London Bridge to a building in Red Bull Alley (close to the site of a famous pre-Restoration theatre) where there was a large and newly built eating house run by the Pieters family. We do not know that he did but we do know that he married Frances, one of the two daughters of the house, sometime in the latter part of 1680. Her father, John Baptist Pieters, had died five years before. He had been born in Ghent, a Flemish Catholic, but had become an English citizen in 1663 and joined the Anglican church. Her mother Amy continued the business after John Baptist's death and, while not rich, was probably financially secure. In marrying a girl from a good watering hole Purcell must have thought she was going to be the perfect and understanding companion for his cosmopolitan lifestyle. As so often, it does not seem to have worked out quite like that.

Chapter 4

A Skilful Hand and an Angelical Voice

Now a settled man with court appointments, a growing public reputation and a soon-to-be pregnant wife, in 1681 the 22 year-old Henry Purcell acquired the first house of his own, presumably affordable with the £8 housing allowance from Westminster Abbey. The home he took was in St Anne's Lane, a dingy little street that runs between Peter Street (now Great Peter Street) and Orchard Street at the edge of the then City of Westminster, close to Tothill Fields west of the Abbey. W.H. Cummings reports the tradition that Purcell was born in the lane. If he was Henry's son this is possible but if he was Thomas's it is less likely and the house referred to was probably Purcell's marital home in the 1680s. Either way the description of it as it was in 1845 by R.W. Whitall gives a good idea of the character of the place. Purcell's house was said to have been the right-hand one of a terrace of three (see picture on page 4). 'The houses are of old red brick. The first door was the back way into the public-house called the Bell and Fish, kept by Mr. Oldsworth, who lost his licence. The second the entrance to the skittle-ground. The third was Purcell's.'

It is likely that Frances stayed at her mother's rather more comfortable home in Thames Street during at least the later part of her pregnancy. The young couple's first child was born in early July and baptised on the 9th in All Hallows the Less, the city of London parish which included the Pieters family's eating house, rather than in St Margaret's or Westminster Abbey as would have been the case had they been resident in St Anne's Lane. Tragically (but all too commonly) the boy, also called Henry, lived for only a few days and was buried in the churchyard on 18 July. Not surprisingly in a year so fraught with emotion, Purcell's music changed from the carefree urbanity of 1680 to a more sombre mood. He concentrated on his work for

The City of Westminster in Purcell's time with Whitehall to the north and Tothill Fields to the south.

Purcell's manuscript of *Swifter, Is, Swifter Flow*, his 1681 Welcome Song.

the Chapel Royal and the Abbey, writing a full ten-item service for the Abbey choir (a rare event for which he was paid an extra 30 shillings). The anthems reflect his state: *O God Thou Hast Cast Us Out; O, Be Thou Our Help In Trouble; Plung'd In The Confines Of Despair.*

In the middle of the upheaval Purcell, along with his brother Edward and great friend the bass John Gostling took the oath under the Test Act in October 1681, formally accepting the rites of the Anglican church and renouncing basic tenets of Catholicism. They were required as public servants to do so – Edward was a Gentleman Usher and Daily Waiter to the King – and those in the royal household were treated with particular suspicion by the generally Whig civic authorities. None the less the timing is odd. The Whigs were at their weakest for years and apart from the fact that Purcell's parents-in-law had once been Catholics there was no reason to prove his Anglican credentials. John Gostling was vicar of a village in Kent so one might have thought his compliance was unnecessary. It may have been merely a matter of prudence or just that slow administrators had finally come round to them.

The gloom is only dispersed by the year's welcome song, *Swifter, Isis, Swifter Flow,* though this may have been written in April when the King returned from holding a Parliament for a week in Oxford (hence the reference to Isis) and before the loss of Purcell's child. The General Election that winter had been the first with candidates formally organized along party lines. The Parliament was held in Oxford to keep it away from the hysterical atmosphere of London. It had failed to resolve the question of Prince James's exclusion from the succession to the King's satisfaction, however, and once it dispersed Charles decided to do without its advice for the future.

That autumn Purcell returned to the theatre, although with nothing like the scale of his work for *Theodosius.* For Killigrew's company at the Theatre Royal – now close to financial collapse – he began a partnership with the comic writer Tom D'Urfey, a Tory at this stage, who was to become one of his most fruitful collaborators. He contributed only one song that survives to *Sir Barnaby Whigg,* or *No Wit Like a Woman's,* a suitably satirical portrait of Shadwell's talents and politics. Purcell's song, *Blow Boreas Blow,* answers Captain Porpuss's demand for 'a Battel, a Siege, a Storm or so' with a suitably nautical setting that became very popular. He was also writing songs that found their way – along with some of the *Theodosius* music – into the third volume of *Choice Ayres, Songs and Dialogues* published by John Playford in 1681. In the course of commending the songs for the composers' ability to set English words Playford took a swipe at the fashion for preferring anything from the continent to home-grown material, an argument which was to intensify after Purcell's death.

'I have seen lately published a large Volum of English Songs, composed by an Italian Master, who has lived here in England many Years; I confess he is a very able Master, but being not perfect in the true Idiom of our Language, you will find the Air of his Musick so much after his Country-mode, that it would sute far better with Italian than English Words...I am sorry it is (in this Age) so much the Vanity of some of our English Gentry to admire that in a Foreigner, which they either slight, or take little notice of in one of their own Nation.'

The offending Italian was Pietro Reggio, Shadwell's friend and lute teacher. It was just at this moment, ironically, that Purcell was taking up the challenge, for that year Corelli's *Sonate de Chiesa*, which were to have an inspirational effect on his English contemporary, were published in Rome and would soon have become available in London.

William Child (1606-1697), Composer, Organist of St. George's Chapel, Windsor and, with Purcell, of the Chapel Royal.

Although Purcell had been a Composer for the Violins for five years and Organist of Westminster Abbey for three, by 1682 he was still not one of the 32 Gentleman of the Chapel Royal like his father and uncle. This meant that his fine singing voice had not been heard in the choir since it had broken from the treble register nine years before. This changed in July when he was appointed in the place of Edward Lowe who had died three days earlier. The official position was as one of the three organists (the others being William Child and John Blow) but they took attendance at the chapel in turns, with one playing, one singing and one absent. Since Child was by then well into his seventies it is likely that Purcell did much more than his strict share of singing. Purcell sang both bass and counter-tenor exceptionally well and became a regular performer of his own music – usually taking the counter-tenor parts since he could rely on John Gostling to do famous justice to the bass line.

Purcell was for once called upon to travel with the King to Windsor that year and despite his promotion the summer months of 1682 were difficult ones for him. Frances was heavily pregnant again and Thomas Purcell was clearly seriously ill. He had handed over his duties as Groom of the Robes in January – with his son Francis taking one of the posts made vacant by the general move around this created – and made his will on 4 June, naming another son, Matthew, as executor. Matthew had already been acting as his representative with powers of attorney for some months. Thomas clung on until the last day of July and two days after his death was buried, like his brother Henry and the other musicians of the age, in the cloisters of Westminster Abbey. He was able to leave his dependants more promises than cash; £5 to each of his sons and the rest of the arrears from his collection of jobs to his wife, along with the house in Pall Mall. For the younger composer it must have been a hard blow. Thomas – whether father or uncle – had been a vital part of his upbringing and was his fellow Composer for the Violins. The Purcell family was large but close; sons, cousins and widows all lived and worked never more than a short walk from each other. Thomas had been the respected head of the family for nearly 20 years.

On 9 August, a week after Thomas's funeral, the Abbey saw a happier Purcell family event; the baptism of Henry and Frances's second child. The boy was named John Baptista after Frances's brother and father. For a few weeks all was well. Purcell was confident enough to inscribe the last page of his manuscript fair-copy book 'God bless Mr. Henry Purcell' on 10 September. The remark may have been as much a plea as an exclamation, though, for the welcome song for the King he settled to compose is less whole-hearted in its rejoicing than usual. If he was doubtful of that blessing his fears were soon confirmed. John Baptista died at the age of two months and was buried on 17 October in the Abbey cloisters, as Thomas had been. The King's arrival at Whitehall from his summer in the country meant that Purcell's welcoming ode was performed on 21 October, only four days after the burial of his son, its opening words now miserably inappropriate for Purcell's state of mind; 'The summer's absence unconcerned we bear / Since you, great Sir, more charming fair appear, / Scattering the mists of faction with our fear.' He turned to the verse anthem, his favourite form in his early years for deep personal statement, to provide a context for his real feelings. *Let mine eyes run down with tears* were the words he set. At the end of the month he also supplied a catch, possibly more than one, for the banquet after the Lord Mayor's show which caught the mood of the moment and confirmed Purcell as, not very surprisingly, a favourite composer for the Tories; *Since The Duke Is Returned We'll Slight All The Whigs.*

The only evidence we have for Purcell's state of mind is the music he chose to write, rather than that which was commissioned either for a special occasion or as a normal part of his court and Abbey duties. Within the confines of the church calendar he could pick the texts for his anthems. He could choose the lyrics of songs which were for concert or private use, rather than for the plays. Solo devotional songs like *Adam's Sleep*, written at this period for use outside church, were popular and useful proof to the general public that his music was not just intended for the frivolities of the court and theatre. And he could write instrumental music. The *Fantazias*, for example, the last of which Purcell wrote in February 1683, were a form outmoded at court but still greatly thought of in more conservative cultured households.

The crossover between amateur and professional music making was much greater than it is now when those with a strong love of music can make do with listening at home electronically. In 17th century London, though, professional musicians and accomplished amateurs like Samuel Pepys, John Evelyn and Roger North were often joined by professional players for a convivial evening. Some enjoyed it more than others of course. Roger North, a lawyer, who had been taught by the composer and master of the viol John Jenkins, was quite at home in professional company. His brother Sir Francis North (who was made Lord Chancellor in 1682 as Lord Guilford) was shyer, preferring to play the bass viol with friends more his standard. Purcell was the one exception and Guilford, who lived in Great Queen Street – just around the corner from the Theatre Royal in Drury Lane – specifically, his brother wrote,

'caused the devine Purcell to bring his Itallian manner'd compositions; and with him on his harpsicord, my self and another violin, wee performed them more than once, of which Mr. Purcell was not a little proud, nor was it a common thing for one of his dignity to be so entertained.'

The Norths were the highest of high Tories, and so the rather snobbish reference to Purcell's dignity (or class) is not surprising. Given the equal pride Roger North took in having known him it was probably harmless and no serious inconvenience. Lord Guilford was known as a moderate and humane man by 17th century standards and a fair lawyer except in political cases when, perhaps remembering his own treatment by a Whig Parliament in the Titus Oates affair, he was conveniently blind to extenuating evidence. In August 1681 he had officiated at the trial and execution of an Oxford joiner, Stephen College, unjustly accused of sedition.

The 'Itallian manner'd compositions' to which Roger North referred were probably the string sonatas that Purcell was writing in response to Corelli's. The sonatas, for two violins, bass and organ or harpsichord formed an ambitious and extensive project for a composer of 24. Although not particularly long – none of the sonatas last for more than seven minutes – they represented a major leap forward in style, taking English music into the European mainstream in a way which its separate church and vernacular theatre works could never do. By accepting the Italian manner, a stricter harmonic language and the discipline of alternating speeds, which were soon to result in the works breaking up into separate movements, Purcell was going further than any of his contemporaries in London who were not themselves Italian. He wrote 22 sonatas in the course of his life but in early 1683 he selected 12 for publication on his own account.

In April the King made his way as usual to the Newmarket races but an accidental fire burnt much of the town and he was forced to return to London early. In the process, as it emerged some weeks later, he frustrated a plan hatched the previous autumn to murder him and James outside Rye House, on the road near Hoddesdon in Hertfordshire. The plot, to settle the succession by murder in favour of the King's illegitimate son, the Duke of Monmouth, turned out not only to have been real (unlike that of Titus Oates) but to have implicated even the Earl of Essex, who escaped execution by slitting his own throat in the Tower of London. By executing Lord Russell and Algernon Sidney more for refusing to disown the principle of insurrection than for any real involvement in the plot, Charles for once in his life badly over-reacted in the way his father had tended to do. The action sowed the seeds of much of the resentment among many sections of society that boiled over to end his brother's reign later in the decade.

Had it been merely a matter of removing a few troublesome politicians there would probably have been little lasting damage. But Charles, heartily sick of the continual unrest of the first years of Whig and Tory antagonism, indulged in the sort of petty oppression and punishment for opinion that had previously been the stock in trade of his extremist Parliaments,

Whig magistrates and, before them, Cromwell. King Charles had retained much of his Restoration popularity principally because he had been able to distance himself from the more vicious deeds of his government and legislature. Now he was implicated, though he was never disliked as much as his brother, and he pursued his enemies by taking the familiar Tory tactic of removing inconvenient local government. In a way that even Henry VIII had not dared, he, in his own interest, revoked and then reissued the ancient charters of the cities and boroughs. Without Parliament meeting and with local government in the hands of his supporters Charles II managed to go further than his father had ever done in establishing absolute monarchy. His admiration for Louis XIV was long-held and genuine. But by 1683 Charles was so dependent on money from France it is doubtful whether he could have resisted influence from Paris even if he had wanted to. Charles however, was not an active ruler, even if he was politically unassailable. He wanted power not to exercise it but to prevent others from making him work. Government was left increasingly to Laurence Hyde (son of his original chief minister, Clarendon), Francis North and to the officious Duke of York – whose first wife had been Hyde's sister. Charles had his mistresses, his horses, his theatre and his music. With the country firmly under the rule of the Tory party, he intended to enjoy them.

His chances of enjoying the theatre, however were now cut by half. Killigrew's company, the King's, had been struggling financially for many years. His sons Thomas and Charles were the active managers of the company by this time and in November 1682 they admitted defeat and allowed Betterton to take them over. He closed Wren's beautiful riverside theatre at Dorset Garden for a time and moved his troupe into the newer and larger house in Drury Lane. He also replaced Charles Hart, Nell Gwynne's mentor who died the following year, with himself as leading man. The theatre, with its royal patent, was now inextricably linked to the court and though it managed to include plays with sharp political comment from both sides, the Whig citizens of London distrusted it.

In 1683 Killigrew, the Master of the Revels, died at the age of 71 and with him went the last substantial link to theatre life before the Civil War, the theatre of Beaumont and Fletcher, Massinger and Ford. His own tragicomedies, mostly written when he was young, had not been as good as some of those by his contemporaries but he was a fine judge of talent in others. The competition between himself and D'Avenant, and between his sons and Betterton, had been intense and often bad-tempered but it had also been productive, pushing both theatres to put on many more new plays than they would have thought necessary or prudent otherwise. The increase in revivals after the two companies merged, and the corresponding drop in opportunities for writers and composers proved the point. Killigrew's love of opera never led to the formation of a proper English opera company as he wanted but he was as responsible as anyone for the quantity and quality of music in Restoration theatre.

The collapse of the King's Company left Purcell high and dry. Although *Theodosius* had been written for Betterton, for his subsequent two contributions he had switched to Drury Lane. Purcell was happy to write music for anyone that asked but in the fevered theatrical politics of the early 1680s, when both companies were facing ruin, such an attitude from a composer who was becoming extremely fashionable at court could be interpreted as defection. We have no direct evidence that Betterton was so petty – he may just have found himself with more composers than he could use in the combined company – but whatever the reason Purcell was, as far as we know, not called upon to write more than one song for the theatre for the following six years; a great waste. The songs that streamed out were instead written for the concert rooms, the court and Playford's publications. He must have missed the theatre for many of the songs, like the famous *Bess of Bedlam,* are intensely dramatic and would have been perfect for the stage.

By May 1683 Purcell was satisfied enough with his set of 12 sonatas to put the following advertisement in the *London Gazette:-*

'These are to give notice to all Gentlemen that have subscribed to the Proposas (sic) Published by Mr. Henry Purcel for the Printing his Sonata's of three Parts for two Violins and Base to the Harpsecord or Organ, That the said Books are now compleatly finished, and shall be delivered to them upon the 11th of June next: And if any who have not yet subscribed, shall before that time Subscribe, according to the said Proposals, (which is Ten Shillings the whole sett) which are at Mr. William Hall's house in Norfolk-street, or at Mr.Playford's and Mr. Carr's Shops in the Temple; for the said Book will not after that time be sold under 15s. the Sett.'

Henry Purcell at 24, as published by him to front his 1683 set of Sonatas.

Vera Effigies HENRICI PURCELL Ætat: Suæ 24.

The pre-publication offer of a third off was a good bargain. Not only were the sonatas beautifully engraved, there was a fine portrait of the composer above the arms of the Purcells of Shropshire (which gives us a clear idea of how he saw his family history) and a helpful note explaining the background to the music and his novel use of Italian tempo markings. Since it is one of very few examples we have of Purcell's own writing and gives a straightforward guide to the speeds he had in mind for each section of the sonatas it is worth quoting in full.

Ingenious Reader.

Instead of an elaborate harangue on the beauty and charms of Musick (which after all the learned Encomions that words can contrive, commends itself best by the performances of a skilful hand,

The manuscript of Purcell's wedding ode for Princess Anne and Prince George of Denmark; *From Hardy Climes and Dangerous Toils of War*.

and an angelical voice:) I shall but say but a very few things by way of Preface, concerning the following Book, and its Author: for its Author, he has faithfully endeavour'd a just imitation of the most fam'd Italian Masters; principally, to bring the Seriousness and gravity of that sort of Musick into vogue among our Country-men, whose humor, 'tis time now, should begin to loath the levity, and balladry of our neighbours: The attempt he confesses to be bold, and daring, there being Pens and artists of more eminent abilities, much better qualify'd for the imployment than his, or himself, which he well hopes these his weak endeavours will in due time provoke, and enflame to a more acurate undertaking. He is not asham'd to own his unskilfulness in Italian Language; but that's the unhappiness of his Education, which cannot justly be accounted his fault, however he thinks he may warrantably affirm, that he is not mistaken in the power of the Italian Notes, or elegancy of their Compositions, which he would recommend to the English Artists. There has been neither care, nor industry wanting, as well in contriving, as revising the whole Work; which had been abroad in the world much sooner, but that he has now thought fit to cause the whole Thorough Bas to be Engraven, which was a thing quite beside his first Resolutions. It remains only that the English Practioner be enform'd, that he will find a few terms of Art perhaps unusual to him, the chief of which are these following: Adagio and Grave which imports nothing but a very slow movement: Presto, Largo, and Vivace, a very brisk, swift or fast movement; Piano, soft. The Author has no more to add, but his hearty wishes, that his Book may fall into no other hands but theirs who carry Musical Souls about them; for he is willing to flatter himself into a belief, that with Such his labours will seem neither unpleasant, nor unprofitable.

Vale'

The works – 'the immediate Results of your Majesties Royall favour, and benignity to me which have made me what I am' – were dedicated to the King and for Purcell too the publication cannot have been unprofitable, since the sonatas needed to be reprinted a few months later.

Much of the rest of 1683 was taken up with official duties at court and major ceremonial occasions. The month after the publication of the sonatas, the Duke of York's daughter Anne married Prince George, brother of the King of Denmark. Neither were particularly good-looking or brilliant but they both had a solid honesty and bravery (and above all a firm Protestantism) which was to make them figures of reassuring stability for many people in the turbulent years ahead. Prince George was an effective soldier. At the time of their marriage,

George was 30 and Anne was 18. Three years earlier she could have been betrothed to her eventual successor, George, Elector of Hanover, but even at 15 Anne did not seem to have been an enticing prospect, a slight for which she never forgave him even though the man she did marry was devoted and faithful. They were married on 28 July and Purcell marked the celebrations with his Ode *From Hardy Climes and Dangerous Toils of War*. The 'hardy climes' were obvious enough. The 'toils of war' referred to George's attempts to fight off the continuing attacks on Danish territory by Charles XI of Sweden. Prince George was a loyal general, though never a great strategist, and the fact that none of the three kings he sought to serve in England ever regarded his talents as more than ordinary was a constant source of bitterness to Anne.

The week before their wedding the leaders of the Rye House Plot were executed. The King promptly left London as soon as the niceties of his niece's marriage were completed. After Windsor he went on to Winchester – the old Saxon capital of Wessex where Wren was building a magnificent palace for him, fit to rival his cousin's at Versailles – then, after a brief visit to London, on to the autumn races at Newmarket. As was by now usual, Purcell was ready with a welcome song for his return and, not surprisingly after a year which had brought the King into greater risk of assassination than at any time since the Civil War, the ode was unashamedly political. *Fly, Bold Rebellion* dismisses the plotters, asserts the supremacy of Charles and brands any opposition to the increasing absolutism as disloyal. Purcell's music is some of his finest of the reign but the reactionary sentiments of the words are not attractive.

His next commission was unlikely to upset anybody, however. A group of music enthusiasts and professionals, including Nicholas Staggins, formed themselves into The Musical Society and arranged for a new work from Purcell and the poet Christopher Fishburn. They provided *Welcome to All the Pleasures*, 'A musical Entertainment perform'd on November XXII, 1683, it being the Festival of St Cecilia, a great Patroness of Music; whose Memory is Annually honour'd by a public Feast made on that day by the Masters and Lovers of Music, as well in England as in Foreign parts.' Perhaps as a prelude to the main event and as a reference to the foreign parts and the continuity of a tradition of Cecilian celebrations Purcell also set a Latin text on the same theme, *Laudate Ceciliam*, using the old notation of 'high

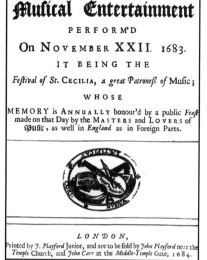

The title page of Purcell's 1683 *Ode to St. Cecilia*, published by John Playford.

A

Musical Entertainment

PERFORM'D

On NOVEMBER XXII. 1683.

IT BEING THE

Festival of St. Cecilia, a great Patroneß of Music;

WHOSE

MEMORY is ANNUALLY honour'd by a public *Feaſt* made on that Day by the MASTERS and LOVERS of Muſic, as well in *England* as in Foreign Parts.

LONDON,

Printed by *J. Playford* Junior, and are to be ſold by *John Playford* near the Temple Church, and *John Carr* at the *Middle-Temple* Gate, 1684.

Manuscript of the Latin ode *Laudate Cecilliam*, also written for the celebrations in November 1683.

value' white notes as it might have been done at the turn of the century. We do not know where the works were performed, though the first part of the ceremonies were held as a service in St Bride's, Fleet Street, so the Latin ode may have been heard there. In later years the festivities took place in Stationer's Hall, with the music being repeated in York Buildings a few days later. We know though that Stationer's Hall was not used in 1683. This first commission having been given in York Buildings alone seems unlikely, firstly because there were no adequate feasting facilities at the concert rooms and secondly because John Evelyn took rooms in the same building 'for the winter, having many important concerns to dispatch, and for the education of my daughters' only five days before and yet makes no mention of what would have been a major event.

A few weeks later Purcell's official workload increased considerably when John Hingston, the Keeper of the King's

Instruments, died. He was probably in his mid-seventies since he had been a chorister at York Minster in 1618. His death meant that only William Child was left of the composers who represented the old post-tudor world of the viol consorts and string fantasies. Purcell had been his unpaid apprentice and then deputy for a decade. On the day of Hingston's funeral, 17 December, Purcell was named as his successor to the salary of £60 per year.

The Thames under ice, transformed into a fairground in 1683.

The winter that year was so cold it almost stopped the city from functioning. The Thames froze – not so remarkable as it would be now because the embanking of it in the nineteenth century has made the river deeper and faster. Nonetheless, although the ice-bound river made the centre of London one great fairground, with booths and sleds and ox-roasts on the Thames, it also stopped the sewers from working. On 1 January Evelyn reported,

'The weather continuing intolerably severe, streets of booths were set upon the Thames; the air was so very cold and thick, as of many years there had not been the like. The small-pox was very mortal.'

By the 9th he was driving across the ice from Westminster to Lambeth in his coach to have dinner with the Archbishop of Canterbury. By the 24th,

'the Thames before London was still planted with booths in formal streets, all sorts of trades and shops furnished, and full of

74

commodities, even to a printing-press, where the people and ladies took a fancy to have their names printed, and the day and the year set down when printed on the Thames: this humour took so universally , that it was estimated the printer gained £5 a day, for printing a line only, at sixpence a name, besides what he got by ballads, &c.'

Most of the royal family strode out onto the ice together and had their names set on one ticket. They were plainly as delighted as everybody else since the little souvenir is still in the archives.

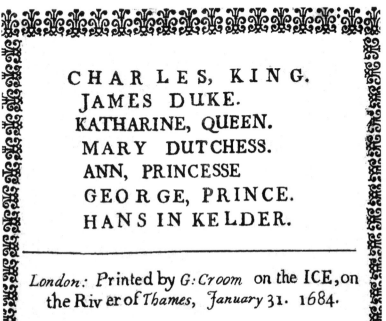

CHARLES, KING.
JAMES DUKE.
KATHARINE, QUEEN.
MARY DUTCHESS.
ANN, PRINCESSE
GEORGE, PRINCE.
HANS IN KELDER.

London: Printed by G: Croom on the ICE, on the River of Thames, January 31. 1684.

The souvenir ticket printed for the Royal family at a booth on the frozen Thames.

One printer who was not so amused was John Playford, whose latest volume of *Songs and Ayres* – including seven by Purcell – was delayed for ten weeks when his press froze. Deliveries to the city became almost impossible because of ice in the Thames estuary and the frozen wharfs. Evelyn itemised the disaster.

'The fowls, fish, and birds, and all our exotic plants and greens, universally destroyed. Many parks of deer were destroyed, and all sorts of fuel so dear, that there were great contributions to preserve the poor alive...London, by reason of the excessive coldness of the air hindering the ascent of the smoke, was so filled with the fuliginous steam of the sea-coal, that hardly could one see across the streets, and this filling the lungs with its gross particles, exceedingly obstructed the breast, so one could hardly breathe. Here was no water to be had from pipes and engines, nor could the brewers and divers other tradesmen work, and every moment was full of disastrous accidents.'

For many , especially the poor, the cold proved fatal. Purcell's family were hit too: his brother-in-law and nephew who lived so close to the river in Thames Street dying in February.

In such conditions Purcell's work as an instrument repairer cannot have been easy. The temperature stresses on the wood of the violins and the metal organ pipes must have caused continual problems. While, like Hingston, he had assistance, there can be no doubt that the more onerous responsibilities of being in full charge made much greater demands on his time. As a result 1684 saw his output slacken compared with the previous years. Since he was out of favour with Betterton – who had just spent some months in Paris at the King's behest trying to import some French opera and had returned only having persuaded the underwhelming Grabu to come back to London – there was precious little theatre work on offer in any case. He did, however, team up with John Blow in helping Henry Playford, John's son, edit his first anthology, *The Theater of Music,* to which Purcell contributed five songs.

For most of the time he concentrated on his duties at the Abbey and the Chapel Royal, composing a string of his best and most enduring anthems, including *Why Do the Heathen so Furiously Rage Together, My Heart is Fixed, O God,* and *Rejoice in the Lord Alway,* using the mastery of string writing which he had now perfected and which King Charles so much appreciated when it livened up his Sunday morning. The King, though, was becoming less of a regular attender at the chapel in Whitehall Palace. When the thaw in April at last made it possible for the country to get back

Winchester Palace, designed by Wren, and Charles II's final great building project, left unfinished at his death and abandoned by his brother. In the 18th century it was used as a barracks.

to normality, Charles quickly left London. With the opposition vanquished and the exchequer in the capable hands of Sidney Godolphin he could pursue matters of more interest. The Council met on Sundays at Hampton Court so it is quite likely that Purcell travelled up river to present his fine new anthems there.

Charles visited the building works at Winchester, anxious to move into his new palace, for which he had stashed away £90,000 in gold from Louis XIV in a secret box. In August Nell Gwynne went with him, causing something of a scandal when one of the royal chaplains, Thomas Ken, demanded that she be thrown out of his house in the Cathedral close. John Evelyn visited the palace a year later, after the work had been stopped.

'It is placed on the side of the hill, where formerly stood the old Castle. It is a stately fabric, of three sides and a corridor, all built of brick, and cornished, windows and columns at the break and entrance of free stone. It was intended for a hunting-house when his Majesty should come to these parts, and has an incomparable prospect.'

Racing at Windsor, 1684; the last race Charles II saw. The picture tells us everything except the name of the winner.

Charles II at the time of his death. This is the effigy which stood by his coffin at his lying in state. The clothes are his own. Today it is exhibited at Westminster Abbey.

Moving on to the Hampshire coast, the King crossed over to the Isle of Wight and sailed on his yacht, called *Fubbs* after the Duchess of Portsmouth who was also rather broad in the beam – broader at least than when she had been a young French lady in waiting 20 years before. John Gostling, the bass for whom Purcell wrote so many of his best solos, accompanied the King on the maiden voyage, which was far from calm, around the north coast of Kent. When Gostling to his relief returned to land and London he made some apposite selections from the scriptures and gave them to Purcell to set. *They That Go Down To The Sea in Ships* was the result; though not one which Charles lived to enjoy Gostling sing.

By the time the King returned to London in the autumn of 1684 it was clear that his health was not good. He had found his usual long walks on the Hampshire Downs at the race meetings too much for his legs. He was well enough, though, to go with his brother James to inspect the troops quartered on Putney Heath in October. It had been a good summer for the King. Politics seemed gentler than they had for years. His Palace was well enough advanced to have its roof on. Newmarket was rebuilt and Charles seemed to be settling into a quiet middle-age of comfortable relations with his mistresses. Thomas Flatman's opening words for Purcell's welcome song at his official return to London were, for once, not too far from the truth; *From Those Serene and Rapturous Joys*.

Before the King came back from Winchester Purcell had been involved in a complicated and acrimonious contest – as only one associated with lawyers can be – at the Temple Church. Roger North had been instrumental in ordering a new organ for the church. Invitations to compete for the work were given to Renatus Harris and Bernard Smith, both of whom built the organs and engaged the best musicians they could find to demonstrate them to the Temple authorities. Harris engaged Giovanni Draghi. Smith opted for Purcell and Blow. Naturally the factions among the Temple lawyers failed to agree on the relative merits of each organ and no decision was reached. Independent judges were appointed, chaired by the infamous Judge Jeffreys who failed to make up his mind for a further four years, a delay which nearly bankrupted both builders. Eventually Smith was awarded the £1,000 for the contract and, though the organ was rebuilt in the nineteenth century, much of his workmanship, which Purcell demonstrated so ably, is still in use.

Charles seemed determined to enjoy life to the full as the winter of 1684 approached. In November a ball was given for the Queen's birthday, said by Evelyn to be the most fabulous since the Restoration, preceded by fireworks and pageants on the river in front of Whitehall Palace. Louis Grabu and John Dryden were hard at work preparing an opera, *Albion and Albanius,* which was to celebrate all the political triumphs of Charles's Tories in the previous years. In December Charles had his first sight of Arab horses when three paraded for him in St James's Park. Imported for the first time, they were on sale for between two and 500 guineas. By January the weather was cold enough to freeze the Thames again, though nothing like on the scale of the year before, and life continued with zest at the palace. Evelyn reported with disapproval on the 25th that 'I saw this evening such a scene of profuse gaming, and the King in the midst of his three concubines, as I have never before seen – luxurious dallying and profaneness.'

On 2 February, Nell Gwynne's thirty-fifth birthday, the King was stricken with a fit as he was getting ready for the day, probably brought on by failing kidneys. Luckily his physician was present and treated him to the best of the knowledge of the time by letting blood. For a few days it proved effective but on 6 February 1685 he relapsed and died, having first taken the last rites, not from the assembled bishops of the Anglican church but from the Catholic chaplain to the Queen, Father Huddleston. It was Charles's last surprise for the nation.

Chapter 5

From Albion to Albanius

'Thus died King Charles II', recorded John Evelyn, who went on to give as dispassionate a summing-up as a King ever received.

'He was a Prince of many virtues, and many great imperfections; debonaire, easy of access, not bloody or cruel; his countenance fierce, his voice great, proper of person, every motion became him; a lover of the sea, and skilful in shipping, not affecting other studies, yet he had a laboratory, and knew of many empirical medicines, and the easier mechanical mathematics; he loved planting and building and brought in a politer way of living which passed to luxury and intolerable expense. He had a particular talent in telling a story, and facetious passages, of which he had innumerable; this made some buffoons and vicious wretches too presumptuous and familiar, not worthy the favour they abused. He took delight in having a number of little spaniels follow him and lie in his bed-chamber, where he often suffered the bitches to puppy and give suck, which rendered it very offensive, and indeed made the whole court nasty and stinking. He would doubtless have been an excellent prince had he been less addicted to women, who made him uneasy, and always in want to supply their unmeasurable profusion, to the detriment of many indigent persons who had signally served both him and his father. ...the history of his reign will certainly be most wonderful for the variety of matter and accidents, above any extent in former ages: the sad tragical death of his father, his banishment and hardships, his miraculous restoration, conspiracies against him, parliaments, wars, plagues, fires, comets, revolutions abroad happening in his time with a thousand other particulars. He was ever kind to me, and very gracious upon all occasions and therefore I cannot without ingratitude but deplore his loss.'

Sighs for Our Late Sovereign King Charles ye 2nd. Purcell's 1685 lament.

Perhaps the greatest tragedy for the country was that although Charles had many children, including plenty of fine sons – whom he acknowledged as his own with dukedoms and places at court – none of them were from his wife, Queen Catherine. This meant that the throne passed, despite the

The Coronation of James II and Mary of Modena in Westminster Abbey, April 1685. The musicians occupy the gallery above the clergy.

Exclusion Acts of the 1670s, to his brother James. In many respects James should have been an excellent choice. He had proved himself an able administrator and admiral, much admired by those who worked with him, and he began by promising 'clemency and tenderness to his people; that, however he had been misrepresented as affecting arbitrary power, they should find the contrary.' This, though, was not the whole story. He lacked Charles's humour and sense of proportion. His early adoption of Catholicism in defiance of political expediency had all the marks of the convert's zeal; his tolerance of opponents and the institutions of the Protestant state was limited to their preparedness to accept nominees happy to adopt his religious views. Tolerance was his stated ideal but only on his terms.

For the first few months little of this was apparent. James was accepted by the established church as its sovereign, whatever his personal beliefs. Preparations for a coronation went ahead as fast as possible. The date was set for St George's Day, 23 April, and Henry Purcell was every bit as involved, indeed more so, than Henry Purcell senior had been at the coronation of Charles II 24 years earlier. As Organist of Westminster Abbey he would have been the senior player in the Abbey for most of the service, though he entered as part of the procession from Westminster Hall as a Gentleman among the basses of the Chapel Royal. As Keeper of the King's

Instruments he was responsible for setting up an auxiliary organ by the altar to accompany the Chapel Royal Choir, who sat separately from the Westminster Abbey Choir and the orchestra. Since the two choirs usually contained seven of the same singers, the Abbey contingent had to be supplemented with deputies for the occasion. As well as the two choirs and two organs the full complement of royal instrumentalists was used; the 24 violins, sackbuts, trumpets and kettledrums placed in a gallery above the clergy and opposite the Abbey choir.

The gentlemen of the Chapel Royal process to James II's coronation.

Nine anthems were sung in all, with Blow, Purcell, William Child and William Turner the main contributors. Only Henry Lawes was represented from composers no longer living; his setting of *Zadok the Priest* in use until Handel's spectacular version in the next century. An anthem of Child's was sung during the procession from the Hall to the church but it was Purcell, as Composer for the Violins, who opened the proceedings in the Abbey when *I Was Glad When They Said Unto Me* (written a couple of years earlier) was sung by the Abbey choir as the King and Queen arrived inside the church. He also closed the main part of the ceremony, this time with a specially composed work for all the string and choral forces at his disposal. At the crowning of the Queen they sang *My Heart Is Inditing*, its spacious rhythms and carefully built-up of textures brilliantly designed to take advantage of the Abbey's grand acoustic and long echo. With the end of the service the choir's duties were over for the day but the orchestra's were just beginning. They transferred back to Westminster Hall for the elaborate coronation banquet (not as elaborate at James's coronation as it had been for his brother, though the catering seems to have been more exotic, taking advantage of the expansion in the produce coming from the new possessions in the tropics during the intervening years). There Nicholas Staggins, as Master of the King's Musick, directed the strings for the tunes that went with the food.

During the previous few months the Purcells had moved out of St Anne's Lane to a house a few streets nearer the Abbey. The new house, in the upper part of what is now Tufton Street – then unpromisingly called Bowling Alley East, just outside the Abbey and School precincts of Dean's Yard – seems to have been larger than the previous one, probably more because Purcell was now taking pupils who boarded with the family than for any grander reasons. With the Protestant Chapel Royal now something of a side-show in the new Catholic court, Purcell's duties were more concentrated on providing secular music and on his job of overseeing the instruments' maintenance. This left more time for songs and catches which, since he was still not being offered any work at the theatre, reached audiences through public concerts, ballad sheets and Playford's publications, which Purcell was now heavily involved in editing.

Prince James (1649-1685), Duke of Monmouth, Charles II's eldest son.

Even for those prepared to accept the emerging new order calculations about the political temperature could go badly wrong. In the last months of Charles II's reign Dryden and Grabu constructed a fully-fledged French-style opera, *Albion and Albanius,* (Charles was Albion and James Albanius) telling in allegory the story of the Restoration and the Exclusion Crisis from an unequivocally Tory viewpoint. It was not to prove a lucky production. King Charles died during the final rehearsals and the theatre then closed for a suitable period of mourning. The première was rescheduled to June and Dryden merely added a few lines covering the death of Albion to bring the script up to date. June proved just as unlucky, though, for the sycophantic opera – for whom the only real audience was the court – opened in the same week that Charles's eldest son, the Duke of Monmouth, marched his under-prepared and ill-led force of West Country tradesmen and labourers against his uncle's seasoned troops commanded by John Churchill, one of the greatest English Generals of any age. At the Battle of Sedgemoor, in Somerset, Purcell's brother Edward – who had relinquished his position in the royal household and obtained a Lieutenant's commission on Charles's death – fought on the

James II (1633-1701).
The naval scene behind
him reflects his career as
Admiral of the Fleet.

King's side. London was not in the mood for frothy operatic allegory and *Albion and Albanius* duly flopped, closing after six performances with a considerable financial loss. In July Purcell's music was heard in the theatre again but his lack of standing was emphasised by the fact that he was only called on to contribute a song sung between acts for Nahum Tate's comedy *The Cuckold's Haven*.

James II did not disband the Chapel Royal or force it to become Catholic. Instead he established his own chapel – opened unnecessarily provocatively on Christmas Day 1686 – staffed by Catholic singers from abroad or those who, like the counter-tenor John Abell, were prepared to switch religions. The new queen, Mary of Modena, also maintained her own musical household, just as her predecessor Queen Catherine had done and still did at Somerset House. Queen Mary preferred to occupy the old Tudor palace of St James's, rather than the suites in Whitehall and so used the beautiful Queen's Chapel. Built there by Inigo Jones, it still serves as a Chapel Royal today. This meant that three out of the four royal choirs, with their organists, were Catholic, leaving only the Chapel Royal – which effectively now only serviced Princess Anne – following the established religion. Its musicians were not required to travel with the court to Windsor and trips to Newmarket and Winchester (where Wren's great Palace was now left incomplete) also ceased with the demise of King Charles.

Apart from being pleasant summer breaks from London for the royal musicians, these migrations had been a useful source of extra fees. In the event they were probably not too upset by these arrangements since James, able financial administrator that he was, consolidated the extra payments into their basic salary. He took steps, aided by a new Parliament especially sympathetic after Monmouth's rebellion, to clear the arrears of the previous reign. Less acceptable must have been the economies made to finance the new Catholic chapel, which meant that James cut back the number of instrumentalists retained by about a third, some 20 posts, over the following two years. Those involved in the private music, instead of the chapel work, were required to travel with the King, however, and Purcell's additional appointment as a Harpsichordist in October 1685 (though this may have been a matter of confirming a position that he had been unofficially occupying for some time) was probably intended by James to make sure that one of the most appreciated keyboard players in London was not left behind because of the religious arrangements.

Purcell's nomination to a new job as a player rather than as a composer does not necessarily mean that he was no longer an official court composer, as many writers on Purcell have assumed. The fact that he continued to write the royal welcome songs suggests that it was understood that he was still employed. Nobody was named in his place, which would have been the case had he actually been sacked. The omission of his composing duties from the rather sketchy job descriptions of King James's court was probably bureaucratic sloppiness. Nonetheless it may well have added to the sense of insecurity felt by this most loyal courtier. Another factor that makes it unlikely that Purcell would have been immediately out of favour with the new regime is the family history of sympathy to Catholicism. Purcell had clearly been under suspicion during the years of the Test Acts and the Exclusion Crisis, given the requirements for public demonstrations of his acceptance of Anglican communion. This is likely to have made him perfectly acceptable to James's initially tolerant administration. Whatever James's tastes in music there were quite enough Italian and French musicians working at his and the Queen's private chapels to make the removal of the established native ones unnecessary. The fact that he confirmed Nicholas Staggins as Master of the King's Musick rather than reinstating Louis Grabu – who was available and must have hoped that *Albion and Albanius* would further his cause – suggests that there were not wholesale changes.

Princess Anne and her husband, Prince George of Denmark, were no substitutes for the voracious musicality of King Charles and were, in any case, considered somewhat minor royals at the time. They were unlikely to require or to inspire Purcell to write the quantity of full-scale orchestrally accompanied anthems that had been needed in the past by the Chapel Royal. As the attention of the King shifted from it, so did its usefulness as a place to present new work to fashionable London society. Under Charles, the Chapel had been a focal point for those who wished to be seen in public close to the King and who were therefore the audience Purcell wished to reach for their patronage, whether directly or through sales of his music. As a result he switched from anthems, with particular liturgical contexts, to religious songs. Because they were sung outside church, they could be enjoyed by followers of both branches of Christianity without their composer being seen to favour either. These religious songs ranged from short verses to the ten-minute dramatic declamation of *Awake and Let Attention Hear* (written in 1685), which prefigures the sort of structure adopted in his cantatas by Bach, who had only been born a few months when it was written. Three years later, in 1688, several of these works found their way into print as part of Henry Playford's two volume collection *Harmonia Sacra*.

Princess Anne (1665-1714), Protestant daughter of James II by his first wife, Anne Hyde. Eventually Queen in her own right.

Whatever Purcell's misgivings about the religious direction of the new reign or his own place in its devotions, he and John Blow were still the King's principal composers. Their secular royal duties continued as before. So, as normal, it was Purcell's job to write the welcome song for James's official return to London in October 1685. He obliged with *Why, Why Are All The Muses Mute?*, which painted the usual flattering picture of James as Caesar routing his enemies, in this case Monmouth, whose

The manuscript of *Why Are All The Muses Mute?*, Purcell's 1685 Welcome Song celebrating James's victory over his nephew, Monmouth.

rebellion Purcell also pilloried in a more satirical way when he set verses by Tom D'Urfey as *The Grasshopper and The Fly*.

For the general public who were not present at the court celebrations or who lived outside the congregational catchment area of Westminster Abbey and the Chapel Royal, Purcell was becoming known principally as a song composer and possibly as a performer, whether on the harpsichord or organ. His songs were beginning to cover a huge scope, remarkable especially since so few of them were originating in the theatre. The popularity of music-meetings, whether regular affairs, like those at Thomas Britton's room above his coal yard, or in the taverns around the country, meant that there was a ready market not just for solo songs but for songs in several parts that were challenging enough to be rewarding but simple enough to be enjoyed by amateurs with tolerable voices, lubricated by several tankards of porter. There were also rounds and canons in unison, which used the simple device of timing to juxtapose words so that they had an entirely different (and usually exuberantly salacious) meaning from the originally innocent lyrics. These 'catches', so called because the voices caught the tune as it was passed around, had been extremely popular for over a century. Composers who were otherwise known for their straight songs took delight, as the great madrigalist Thomas Morley said in 1597, in writing songs 'designed for mirth and recreation'. Thomas Ravenscroft collected hundreds of 'pleasant roundelayes and delightful catches' in the early years of the 17th century and John Playford had been publishing catches since 1652 when he and John Benson printed the first edition of John Hilton's collection *Catch That Catch Can, A Choice Collection of Catches, Rounds and Canons for 3 or 4 voyces* brought out to satisfy the demand for songs to relieve the earnestness of the puritan Cromwellian regime.

By 1685 Hilton's collection was superseded by a new edition, retaining the first part of the title but including new pieces by Blow, Michael Wise, Thomas Aldrich and 12 by Purcell. The catches could be simply romantic or thoroughly mucky or sometimes political, like *Now England's Great Council's Assembled*, but they were the musical part of the coffee-house and tavern culture that made governmental and church attempts at controlling public opinion irrelevant. Purcell was a first-rate catch composer and he took full advantage of the taste of the time for humour that is even now considered too robust for modern listeners. Since so few pubs now have singing and music has to be performed by professionals to a paying audience in solemn concerts, Purcell's rougher songs are either not heard at all or given in gentrified versions, which make them pretty trifles and much less fun. In an age of adult videos it is sad that there are, at the time of writing, no recordings of Purcell's lustier songs in their impolite versions. This reduction of bawdry to mild double-entendre means that there is a false view of Purcell's output. He is classed as a nice classical composer. In fact he had a far broader appeal. The songs that had appeared in 1684 in the two volumes of *The Theatre of Music*, combined with his catches and his later music for the theatre meant that for his contemporaries in London he was primarily a popular writer, closer to Gershwin in the early part of the twentieth century but without parallels now (Bernstein was probably the only recent musician to bridge musical categories with anything like the same competence).

1686 was a year of uneasy consolidation mixed with personal and professional sadness for Purcell. Once again, in August, Frances Purcell gave birth to a son and the traditional family names were continued with Thomas but once again he was soon buried in the Abbey cloisters. However high the infant mortality rate the constant round of pregnancy, hope and immediate grief must have put a strain on the marriage. Purcell was now 27, a mature age in those days, in as secure employment as was possible at court and he would have hoped to be the father of a thriving family. Without theatre work and trips to Newmarket to distract him, he was probably spending more time at home than for many seasons, teaching his boarding pupils and working on songs for publication.

He was hardly overstretched for work. He had time enough (and he was no doubt glad of the fee of a couple of pounds) to join John Blow and two others for a day as judges of a new organ by Bernard Smith at St Catherine Cree and auditions for a new organist to play it. For a musician of Purcell's eminence, teaching could be a lucrative sideline. Students, however, were not necessarily more reliable in their payments than the exchequer. In November 1686 Purcell felt compelled to write to the Dean of Exeter over an outstanding bill of £27 left unpaid by a Mr Hodg since June.

The professional sadness came with the death at the end of the year of his (and Child, Lawes, Blow and Locke's) principal publisher, John Playford, aged 63. For the composers of the

A page from Purcell's book of fair copy manuscripts. At the foot is *Here's to Ye, Dick*, one of his tavern songs of the 1680s.

John Playford (1623-1686),
Purcell's publisher.

Commonwealth and Restoration periods Playford had been the perfect partner. Brought up as one of a long line of Norwich stationers and for many years Clerk of the Temple Church and a Vicar-choral of St Paul's Cathedral, he had combined a thorough knowledge of publishing with a practitioner's instinct for good music. Although he had handed over the business to his son Henry two years before, he was plainly much missed and Purcell commemorated him in a fine *Elegy* with words by Nahum Tate.

1687 cannot have been any easier for Purcell or for his wife. She was securely pregnant again by the end of 1686, a condition that must have seemed to have become almost permanent but with no family as reward. Purcell's finances were less solid than ever. Without extra travel payments and with nothing coming in from the theatre he was thrown back on his main court post as Keeper of the Instruments and on fees for publishing and performing in the King's Private Music. Even this was proving unreliable, however, since despite his good administrative start, James II's Treasury was turning out to be just as hard to extract money from as his brother's had been. This behaviour was perhaps symptomatic of the general insensitivity with which James and his officials were beginning to treat the Anglican establishment. In theory James was keen to promote toleration, not to usurp the order of the state. He publicly opposed Louis XIV's repeal of the Edict of Nantes, which had protected the Huguenots from persecution, and made sure that his Toleration Act included the rights of non-conformists like the Quakers (led by Sir William Penn) as well as his own Catholic sympathisers. The Pope and the English Cardinal Howard both advised James to move cautiously and pragmatically. Had James been Charles, this advice would probably have been cleverly followed. James, though, was an impatient man for whom issues were always clearly delineated. For or against were the only two possible positions. Increasingly he was deciding that Anglicans were against him and while he was smart enough to know that they were too powerful to oppose, forming the major part of his own Tory support, they could at least be ignored, replaced or pushed into irrelevance.

For some High Tories like the poet laureate John Dryden the move to the King's religion was politically sensible and not too difficult, though it did mean jettisoning opinions published during the 1670s and early eighties. Dryden paraded his new faith by translating a life of St Francis Xavier in 1686 and the next year publishing his long poetic allegory *The Hind and The*

Aphra Behn (1640-1689), London's foremost woman Restoration playwright and novelist.

Panther, reconciling the positions of the Catholic Church (the hind) and the Church of England (the panther), giving the Crown as their common pillar and the Whigs as their shared enemies. It was a subtle attempt and an elegant political and religious doctrine that combined moderation and Tory intolerance of opposition in equal measure but it can have convinced very few outside James's court, any more than *Albion and Albanius* had done two years before. For other loyal Tory servants of the Crown, however, like Purcell, Blow and the writers Nahum Tate and Aphra Behn, support for the King did not lead to conversion or even approval of his religion, even when they dutifully praised him as the rightful Caesar in public odes. Gradually this led not to their exclusion (except for Behn) but to their absence from positive favour.

For Purcell both family and financial matters were brought to a head in the second week of June 1687. Frances gave birth to another son on the 9th, this time named Henry which had, after all been a lucky name for surviving Purcell children for most of the century. During the same week Purcell petitioned the Treasury for his back pay and it was duly passed from one department to the other on the 10th. The bill came to £137 for maintenance, tuning and repair of the Chapel Royal organ (£40 for putting it back into serviceable condition and £20 per annum for its upkeep thereafter), his own salary and expenses and the settlement of invoices already delivered. The bill also contains some interesting details about the cost of performances at court and its surprising lack of instruments, as well as the care Purcell took in preparation. For each song given before King James he charged £4. This sum was just for performance (presumably its composition was covered by his salary as Composer in Ordinary). It had to include the cost of hiring, transporting and tuning a harpsichord – which one might have expected the Palace of Whitehall to possess – and fees for three rehearsals. Sadly Purcell does not specify which songs these were or for how many voices. But his invoice does at least make clear that however flowery the language of royal warrants, musicians in the late 17th century did not perform to the King for free. Singers and players demanded a proper rate for the job.

If Purcell expected his detailed and forcefully worded accounts to be dealt with promptly he was disappointed. Nothing was done for another six months. It was just such cavalier treatment of loyal members of the household that increasingly turned them against the government, especially as they saw money being lavished by James on the more fashionable Catholic chapel to attract musicians from Italy and other continental countries. Purcell and Blow must have felt much as the same as the previous generation had done when Charles II had passed over those loyal to his father's tastes in favour of those composers able to write in an eclectic French style.

Once again September proved to be a bitter month as the Purcell's latest child died and was taken to the Abbey cloisters, though Frances conceived again almost simultaneously. Grieving and unpaid Purcell must have found the writing of that autumn's welcome song less than congenial. *Sound the Trumpet, Beat the Drum* was, despite the composer's circumstances, one of his most magnificent in the genre; so much so that he used the music twice more – as a welcome for William III and (in the case of the splendid Chaconne which may have allowed for some celebratory choreography) in *King Arthur*. In James's reign the autumn ode had a double significance in that his return to London and the seat of

Sound the Trumpet, Purcell's 1687 Welcome Song for James II.

government from summer wanderings also coincided with his birthday on 14 October. Impressive as Purcell's ode was, James's birthday in 1687 (his forty-fourth) was not celebrated too exuberantly outside the Palace. The usual London manner of public rejoicing, lighting bonfires in the streets, was banned, partly because it was also the traditional way of signalling popular rebellion and partly to seem even-handed in that the ban also extended to the 5 November Guy Fawkes fires. James was understandably keen to play down memories of Catholic plots against his grandfather.

It is possible that the cut in manpower of the officially retained royal musicians was making the administration of court music more difficult. While the singing establishment was probably coping, the instrumental players had to service the Theatre Royal, court functions, the King's tours to Windsor and sometimes beyond and both the Chapels Royal. It seems as though Nicholas Staggins had decided to concentrate on James's requirements. This raised resentments in Whitehall where the Lord Chamberlain had to remind Staggins the week after the King's birthday to arrange for players to be present at the Protestant Chapel Royal when Princess Anne (who was feeling isolated and under increasing threat at court, yet was not allowed to leave the country) was attending on Sundays.

Purcell's own position in the religious debate seems also to have been hardening. He returned to writing for the Chapel Royal (maybe it was for a performance of his that the members of the King's Violins were required). There was quiet defiance in the anthems. In *Sing Unto God, O Ye Kingdoms* he cleverly gave the main bass soloist music which very few except John Gostling would have been able to sing. Since Gostling was an Anglican priest he would not have been able to perform in the King's private chapel and Purcell's music could only have been heard in the official church on the other side of the Palace garden. Several of the anthems written during this and the following year were similarly composed with Gostling in mind, clearly indicated in a manuscript book kept by the singer.

Purcell adopted the position his family had always done since the Civil War; loyalty to the Crown, sympathy for high church traditions but firm adherence to the Church of England. He demonstrated this quietly but publicly by spending the autumn of 1687 editing the contributions, including 12 of his own, to *Harmonia Sacra*, which Henry Playford advertised in November and registered at Stationer's Hall the following month. The volume was dedicated to Dr. Ken, the Bishop of Bath and Wells, who was an outspoken opponent of James's Catholicism and fearless of royal displeasure. Two years earlier, when he was still only a chaplain to King Charles, it had been Ken who had thrown Nell Gwynne out of his house in the Winchester Cathedral close. It seems likely that the choice of devotional songs for the volume was Purcell's own for it is something of a tribute to his teachers, Blow, Locke and Humfrey, all of whom (along with his fellow chorister William Turner) are included. Playford was openly trying to offer a retrospective selection of serious music for use outside the church which declared the vitality of Anglican music without being offensive to the Catholic regime or inaccessible to dissenters. It was also intended to balance the large number of lighter anthologies which were now available. In these Purcell continued to be just as well represented. Playford published more songs and catches during the year, as did John Carr, whose fancy Latin titles – *Comes Amoris* and *Vinculum Societatis* – did little to conceal the popular nature of the contents.

Even these sources of income came close to being denied to Purcell and his fellow Anglican composers when in November John Abell, the counter-tenor who was very much the star of the English recruits to James's Catholic Chapel, tried to revive the monopoly on music printing enjoyed by William Byrd (also a Catholic) at the turn of the century. At a time when the government was making a stern effort to crack down on unlicensed printing presses, such a monopoly would have made it almost impossible for royal employees like Purcell to have had their music published by anyone else. This would have subjected everything that reached the public to Catholic censorship. Thankfully Abell's request was not granted but it must have caused more than a few sleepless nights.

In December 1687 the Treasury finally took some action over Purcell's claim for fees and expenses. But there was not exactly a sense of urgency. The bill was passed to the Dean of the Chapel Royal, the Bishop of Durham, for investigation. Even then the traditional Whitehall delaying tactics were well established, it seems. Purcell reminded those at the Chapel Royal of his quality by writing a new anthem for Christmas, *Behold, I Bring You Glad Tidings*. It was the only piece of Christmas music he wrote, reflecting the relatively minor place – compared to Lent, Easter and Michaelmas – this festival had in the musical calendar until the German customs were adopted in England in the nineteenth century.

There was another chance to offer official thanksgiving early in January when it was announced that Mary of Modena (then nearly 30 years old) was pregnant. Prayers were ordered to be said in all churches in London and villages within a 12 mile radius on 15 January and Purcell was required to compose a suitable anthem. He obliged with *Blessed Are They That Fear The Lord*. Psalm 128, from which the text was taken, referred to everything that James and Mary would have wished to hear. It mentioned their happiness, her fruitfulness (by no means then established), the start of a long line of children and peace for the country. Given Mary's history of miscarriage the success of the preganancy can hardly have been certain in January with six months to wait until the baby was due. Nonetheless her condition gave James a new sense of confidence that a straightforward succession was possible and a belief that his moves to re-establish royal, and eventually state, Catholicism were being divinely approved. In reality a line of children did emerge but far from bringing peace and security they were the cause of tragic warfare between England and Scotland for the next half century and of persecution and intolerance in Ireland which still resonates today. Perhaps it says something about Purcell's place in the national conscience that his music was used both to celebrate the Catholic succession and, with his setting of the tune *Lilliburlero*, to signal its defeat.

By early 1688 men in Purcell's position – royal servants with their loyalty divided between church and Crown – were justifiably nervous of James's increasingly effective campaign to destabilise the establishment. He moved with the thoroughness and an understanding of the mechanisms of power which would have done credit to any Soviet leader. Agents were despatched throughout the country with full powers to ensure that all towns and boroughs were so managed that they were only capable of electing new Members of Parliament supportive of the government. It was work started by Charles II but more subtly carried out by his brother. By March more than twelve hundred local officials, from magistrates and freemen to sheriffs and tax collectors, had been sacked and replaced. James did not resort to either arbitrary persecution or bribery. His was a careful plan for political management, ensuring that those able to deliver his policies, whether they be dissenters, Catholics or Whigs, were in legitimate control of all sections of local government able to influence an election. He was turning politics on its head. The Tory interest which had backed him throughout the Exclusion Crisis and guaranteed his accession was also the Anglican interest which opposed his over-riding determination to reform the state religion, first by allowing toleration so that all citizens could play a full part in public life (for which there was significant support) and then by securing a Catholic succession (for which there was not). Throughout most of 1688 James was able to carry forward his policy of wholesale sackings largely because the arrogant Tory office holders had made themselves so unpopular. Many of them were the same local gentry who had opposed Cromwell and quashed dissent after the Restoration. They and their clerical allies had only been installed a few years before when royal interests were very different.

Purcell was perhaps lucky that, apart from his more than acceptable royal odes and anthems, he was not called upon to express either support or censure for James. Ironically his career was showing signs of moving forward again. In March after the Bishop of Durham had reported back to the Treasury, he was finally paid the full amount for which he had petitioned the previous year and confirmed in his post as Keeper of the Instruments (Purcell had cleverly asked for a salary four pounds less per annum than in the previous reign). At much the same time his friend Tom D'Urfey commissioned him to write a substantial number of theatre songs for the first time in six years. The eight songs he contributed to *The Fool's Preferment* or *The Three Dukes of Dunstable* in April did not save the play – it seems to have been the most spectacular flop of the decade for D'Urfey, even though it is one of his cleverest pieces - but 'I'll Sail Upon the Dog Star,' written for Will Mountfort who played the madman Lionel, became one of Purcell's most enduring songs. In May, the same month that it and the rest of the play's material was published, four more songs were issued in the second volume of Playford's *Banquet of Music* and – much more importantly – Frances gave birth to a healthy daughter.

The title page for the first edition of D'Urfey's *The Fool's Preferment* (1688), which gave Purcell his first chance to write for the theatre in six years.

Chapter 6

Victorious Charms

Less than two weeks after the Purcell's latest baby was born the Queen had a son. Its timing was so convenient for James, coming only two days after he had sent seven Bishops to the Tower for refusing to read his declaration of liberty of conscience from their pulpits, that many (including at first Princess Anne) refused to believe its legitimacy. For years the story that a substitute baby had been smuggled into the Queen's bedchamber in a warming pan was used as anti-Jacobite propaganda. Most of those who were in a position to judge at the time accepted the child's parentage, however.

Significantly, although he had written music to celebrate the pregnancy, Purcell was not called upon to provide anything for the celebrations for the new Prince of Wales's birth. That function was performed in elaborate entertainments at Whitehall by members of James's Catholic household. However the Purcell family's carefully judged position was paying dividends. Henry's younger brother Daniel benefited from the turmoil of the King's appointments when he was made Organist of Magdalen College Oxford in the spring by the new President, the Catholic Bishop Gifford. Daniel was not a Catholic but was already making a name as a composer of songs and was from one of the most loyal families of royal servants. It was an inspired move on Gifford's part and Daniel proved acceptable to the College long after the controversy over his patron (who was dismissed by James as a desperate measure of conciliation in the autumn) had died away. He relinquished the post in 1695, when he moved back to London at his brother's death. The active relations between the English court and the Vatican, meanwhile, of which music was an inevitable diplomatic tool, were bringing Henry Purcell's music to the attention of Italy, and in particular to Corelli, who dominated the Roman musical scene. While without copyright legislation Purcell received no financial benefit from the

Daniel Purcell, Henry's younger brother. After a few years as Organist at Magdalen College, Oxford, he came back to London and continued the family tradition of writing for the theatre.

circulation of his works abroad, it did strengthen his position at home. It meant that the large number of Italian musicians now gathered round James arrived knowing that England had at least one contemporary composer (and since Blow's works were also circulating widely, probably two) of international stature.

However Purcell's music had the disadvantage for international audiences that it was in English and almost entirely vocal, despite his old official title as Composer for the Violins. With the exception of three Latin settings it would have been inaccessible to Catholic audiences abroad. Only the *Sonatas*, which he had published five years earlier, were likely to be readily available overseas. Perhaps because Nicholas Staggins monopolised the orchestra, Purcell seems to have made no effort, despite his professed fascination with Italian music, to have attempted the concerto grosso or violin, flute and oboe concertos, which were becoming the most fashionable form on the continent. Why not remains a mystery. He had the time and the popularity of music meetings, whether in York Buildings or elsewhere, provided plenty of opportunity. Equally the large number of Italian musicians in London, both instrumentalists and composers, guaranteed that he cannot have been ignorant of European developments. It is possible that English publishers fought shy of works that were beyond the scope of small amateur chamber groups and that orchestral music not performed and preserved in the theatre had little chance of being printed. It is equally possible that successive fires in the Palace of Whitehall could have destroyed important manuscripts which Purcell had lodged there. Purcell was a composer who wrote on demand and who never travelled beyond his places of employment. Perhaps, therefore, the incentive to tackle new cosmopolitan forms was lacking. For a composer of Purcell's curiosity and inventiveness this seems unlikely, though.

At some time – perhaps, given its text, in the spring – he wrote another full anthem with strings for Gostling and the Chapel Royal: *The Lord is King, The Earth May Be Glad*. But in the summer of 1688, with a child at last thriving, Purcell was hardly working at full capacity. Instructions that the royal musicians were henceforth to provide music for the Queen's maids as well as their mistress was perhaps a response to their under-use by the royal family as much as an onerous and insensitive new duty. Princess Anne and Prince George were taking the waters in Tunbridge Wells. The infant Prince of Wales was in Richmond. The King, who had lost his attempt to indict the rebellious bishops and who was dangerously isolated from opposition opinion, was aware for the first time that his position was precarious and spent time building up the army. He had withdrawn regiments from the service of his nephew and son-in-law William in Holland and forbade visits to The Hague. The new interest of Anglican politicians in William's position was beginning to bear uncomfortable resemblance to the comings and goings across the channel before Charles's Restoration 29 years earlier. James billeted the troops, including Purcell's brother Edward, serving in Colonel Trelawney's regiment, on Hounslow Heath as he had each year of his reign as an insurance against revolt in London. While Princess Anne and her husband were away the Chapel Royal was being renovated and Purcell perhaps took the opportunity to repair the organ as he had now been paid to do. His duties at Westminster Abbey were in any case light and teaching would not have occupied him for any significant proportion of his time.

Realising that the political situation was fast moving out of his control, King James returned to London in mid September, obviating the need for the usual October welcome song from Purcell. By the time the King's birthday came round in October the court was in far too much of a panic for elaborate

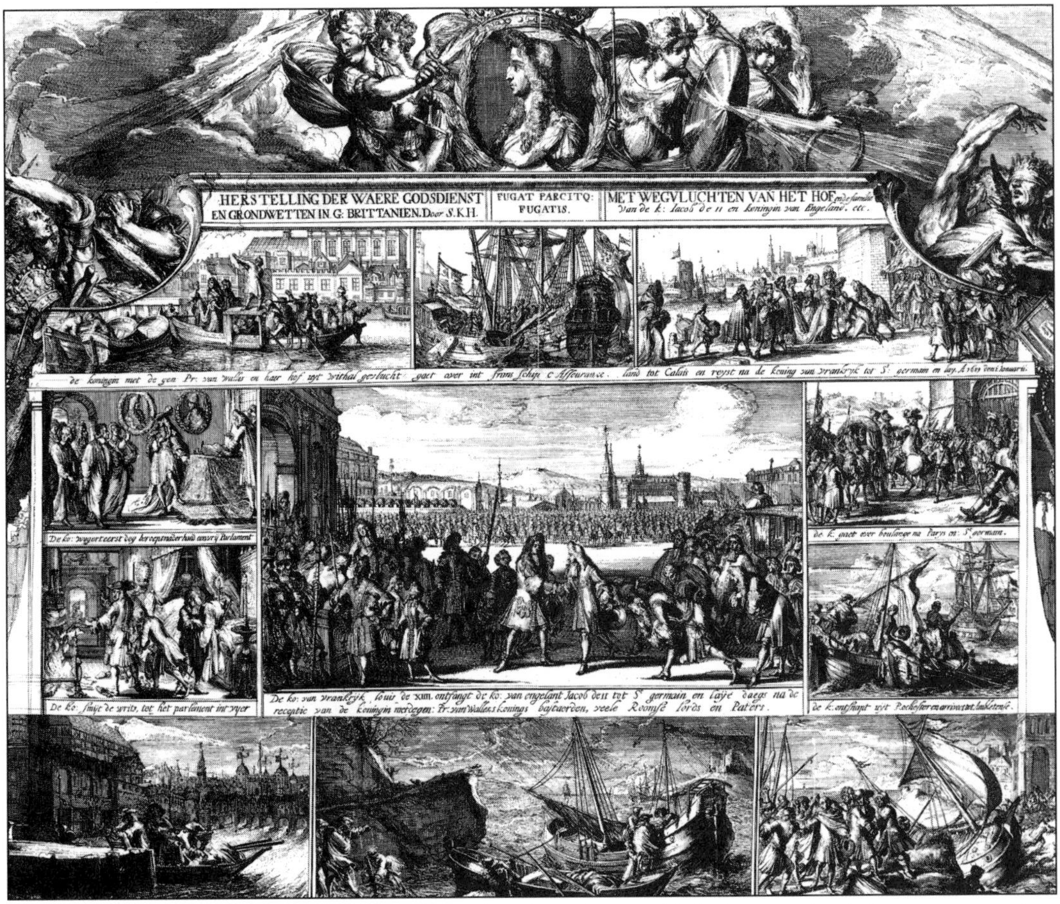
HERSTELLING DER WAERE GODSDIENST
EN GRONDWETTEN IN G: BRITTANIEN.
FUGAT PARCITQ: FUGATIS.
MET WEGVLUCHTEN VAN HET HOF

A Dutch engraving showing the muddled business of James II's flight to France.

celebrations. The invasion which James had been expecting finally happened when William landed at Torbay with unintentional but appropriate timing on 5 November, William's thirty-eighth birthday and the anniversary of the Gunpowder Plot. During the next month the King's forces gradually deserted him and one escape attempt to France in early December was foiled by over-zealous Kentishmen who mistook him for a Jesuit. Two weeks later William entered London, first making sure that James escaped safely. He had no desire to be seen seizing the throne. With true Dutch patience, however, he made sure that he was in the right place when the throne was left unoccupied. For the musicians at Westminster throughout this almost bloodless revolution, there was little to do. Purcell was occupied by two slight works, an anthem – *Blessed Is the Man That Feareth the Lord* – for Founders Day at Charterhouse School, premièred on the Wednesday of the week after James first fled London and before he returned in embarrassed pomp the following Sunday – and an *Elegy* on the death of Thomas Farmer, one of the few native composers attached to James's Catholic Chapel.

The fact that the text for this *Elegy,* written quickly and when loyalties were confused, was by Nahum Tate is, I believe, of great significance. Purcell had time on his hands and no outlet for his work. The theatre was effectively barred to him by Betterton's indifference. Normal musical life in London was at a standstill. The time was ripe for Tate and Purcell to take forward a project which they may have been preparing ever since Dryden and Grabu's *Albion and Albanius* two years earlier. This was *Dido and Aeneas,* the work that has come to have the same status for English opera that Monteverdi's *Orfeo* has for Italian: not the first work in the genre but the best of the first and the only musical stage work from London in the 17th century to have found a consistent place in the operatic repertory since. Ironically it was in fact never staged by a professional company in Purcell's lifetime or, quite, in that century.

There are as many different theories about when *Dido and Aeneas* was written as there are writers on Purcell. There is only one undisputed fact and that is that Tate's libretto was published at the end of 1689. There would have been little point in publishing the libretto too long after news of the performance, especially since Tate's volume of *New Poems* were ready for the press the following year. For Purcell and Tate to have been writing a short opera for a girl's school in Chelsea during 1688 makes great sense. Tate, seven years older than Purcell, was an ambitious man whose reputation as a theatrical poet was lagging behind Dryden (who was stripped of his Laureateship even before William and Mary were given the throne), Shadwell, D'Urfey and the ailing Aphra Behn. With the political situation – and therefore the state of patronage – in such disarray Tate and Purcell needed a vehicle to bring them back into the limelight. Purcell was in danger of being considered only as a composer of songs and of music for the court. He would also have been glad of the chance to be able to compete with the foreign composers in London in a proper opera, however small the scale (and without the interference of Betterton), at a time when the talents of native composers needed proclaiming. Since there was no chance of a through-sung opera being commissioned by Betterton's United Company – which in any case was in abeyance during the latter part of 1688 because of the unrest – Priest's school offered a risk-free alternative.

Given the modern status of *Dido and Aeneas,* its original commission for a school production has been derided as a waste

Thomas Betterton (1635-1710), actor-manager and adaptor of *Dioclesian*.

100

of a great work on amateur forces. This is to misunderstand the usefulness to Tate and Purcell of such a neutral venue and to underestimate the importance of the school itself. Josias Priest and his wife had been running a successful school for young gentlewomen for about 20 years. At first it had occupied a site in Leicester Fields – just north of the royal mews (now Trafalgar Square) but, as this area began to be developed in 1680, he moved the school to a larger house at Cheyne Walk, Chelsea (close to what is now Battersea Bridge but was then a ferry landing) that had once belonged to Richard Portman, Organist of Westminster Abbey under Charles I. The school rapidly became the most fashionable place for educating the daughters of the aristocracy. Music had a vital place in its curriculum. Five years before *Dido*, Blow's *Venus and Adonis* – the masque he wrote for Molly Davis and her daughter by Charles II, Mary Tudor – was restaged there after its Oxford court performance and it is quite possible that Purcell taught girls from the school. Chelsea already had its reputation as a pleasant rural suburb colonised by artists, writers and musicians who could meet and have a shave at Don Saltero's Coffee House in Danvers Street. The opening of the Royal Hospital at the other end of the village in 1689 was to make the area even more fashionable. Priest himself had been the most famous English dancer of his generation in the 1670s and though he did not hold an official post at court was revered as a dancing master. For Priest too it was a good moment to remind the court of his credentials, since the choreographer's post was held by a Catholic who was dismissed during the winter.

Given the exigencies of school timetables, the need for rehearsals with the professionals who were probably brought in for the four major singing parts (Dido, Aeneas, Belinda and the Enchantress) and above all the preparations for the 17 dances (for only a few of which we still have Purcell's music) that Tate included in the libretto to give Priest suitable opportunity to show off the girls' skill, the music must have been ready during the winter if it was performed in the summer of 1689. After March Purcell was far too busy with other music to have had time to do more than tinker with the score, even though he was a fast writer. This means that Tate is most likely to have been working on the libretto during the summer and autumn of 1688 when politics hung in the balance. This would explain why the subject matter, inspired by his own play *Brutus of Alba* or *The Enchanted Lovers* of ten years before (which he had originally intended to be called *Dido and Aeneas*), avoids the obvious

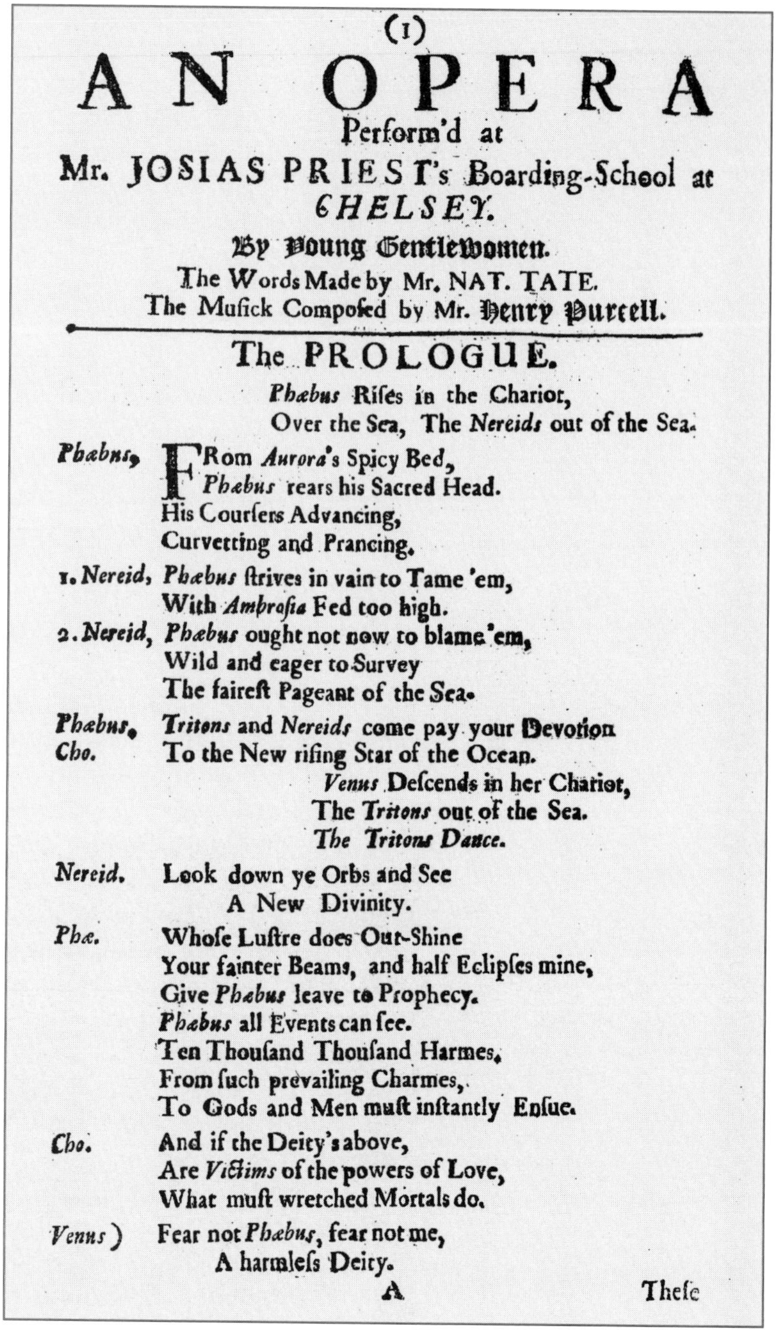

The opening page of Nahum Tate's libretto for *Dido and Aeneas*, printed at the end of 1689.

(1)

AN OPERA

Perform'd at

Mr. JOSIAS PRIEST's Boarding-School at

CHELSEY.

By Young Gentlewomen.

The Words Made by Mr. NAT. TATE.

The Musick Composed by Mr. Henry Purcell.

The PROLOGUE.

Phœbus Rises in the Chariot,
Over the Sea, The *Nereids* out of the Sea.

Phœbus, FRom *Aurora*'s Spicy Bed,
Phœbus rears his Sacred Head.
His Coursers Advancing,
Curvetting and Prancing.

1. *Nereid*, *Phœbus* strives in vain to Tame 'em,
With *Ambrosia* Fed too high.

2. *Nereid*, *Phœbus* ought not now to blame 'em,
Wild and eager to Survey
The fairest Pageant of the Sea.

Phœbus, *Tritons* and *Nereids* come pay your Devotion

Cho. To the New rising Star of the Ocean.

Venus Descends in her Chariot,
The *Tritons* out of the Sea.
The Tritons Dance.

Nereid. Look down ye Orbs and See
A New Divinity.

Phæ. Whose Lustre does Out-Shine
Your fainter Beams, and half Eclipses mine,
Give *Phœbus* leave to Prophecy.
Phœbus all Events can see.
Ten Thousand Thousand Harmes,
From such prevailing Charmes,
To Gods and Men must instantly Ensue.

Cho. And if the Deity's above,
Are *Victims* of the powers of Love,
What must wretched Mortals do.

Venus) Fear not *Phœbus*, fear not me,
A harmless Deity.

A These

political allegory of *Albion and Albanius*. Purcell and Tate would have learnt their lesson from Dryden and Grabu's experience. Although in the event it could have been interpreted as unfortunate that the action was about a prince who arrives from across the sea, forms a short-lived joint monarchy and then leaves the Queen to love-lorn suicide, the site of the performance at the school rather than the Theatre Royal probably neutralised the potentially difficult situation. Surely

too, if (as Maureen Duffy argues) the newly-crowned queen, Mary, attended the first performance while William was away, she would have – as all have since – been won over by the beauty and desolation of Dido's lament.

For a school performance the subject matter was perfect. It had a small number of central characters, plenty of scope for choruses and dancers and was short. However, even though the score that survives lasts for under an hour it was still Purcell's most extended work to date. But perhaps what most appealed was the opportunity to set words that could exploit the melodic directness and simplicity that had been coming into his musical style in the previous few years. The lilt of the dances, the insistent rhythm of a ground bass, the folksong-like humour of the sailor's songs were all characteristics that had been growing more important since he had been devoting less time to church music for the court and turned instead to songs and popular catches. More than any other respected composer of the time he was beginning to find the touch that made his music reach out alike to the sophisticated listener and those that just wanted to hear a good tune.

Mary Stuart and William of Orange accept the offer of the Crown at the Banqueting House in Whitehall, February 1689.

Between James II's flight in December and his daughter's arrival from The Hague in February there was an anxious interregnum while it was decided whether William or Mary, or both, would reign. They had equal claims to the throne, though Mary's was the more direct, and while it was clear that William would not be content as a mere consort it was equally the case that the English preferred to be ruled by one of their own. However it was certain that there was to be a new direction and that the difficult position of the Chapel Royal composers under James would be eased whoever succeeded him. I believe it was in these weeks that Purcell composed one of his most popular anthems for the chapel, *O Sing Unto the Lord a New Song*. The words are those of rejoicing and relief as well as a clear statement that the Protestant version of the monarchy was favoured in heaven;

'Let the whole earth stand in awe of him. Tell it out among the heathen that the Lord is King, and that it is he who hath made the round earth so fast that it cannot be moved, and how he shall judge the people righteously, Alleluja'.

The anthem is dated 1688 but since under the old style dating system still then in use, new year was not marked until April, it could well have been appropriate for January. In that month Frances Purcell, who at last had a child past the most dangerous early weeks of infancy, conceived again.

It was in these months too that Purcell would have been at work on preparing harpsichord pieces, including seven by himself, for publication as *The Second Part of Musick's Hand-maid*, which appeared in May. There was a sign of the times in the title of one of the pieces, *Sefauchi's Farewell*, a tribute to the famous Italian castrato Siface who had been one of the foreign virtuosi at James's court. Taken along with Purcell's *Elegy to Thomas Farmer* it suggests that relations between the musicians at the Chapel Royal and the Catholic chapel round the corner were not all bad. Purcell's principal post with James was as a harpsichordist in the private music and it is somewhat surprising that he was publishing or preserving so few instrumental works. It reinforces the impression that the main focus of his attention as a composer continued to be the voice.

There must have been a considerable sense of déjà vu at court in the early months of 1689. For the second time in four years there was a new King in February, with a coronation planned for early April. And in each case the change meant a swap of religious practice and with it wholesale sackings in the royal household. Many Stuart loyalists among the Anglicans, including Purcell, felt ambivalent about the change. Surprisingly he does not seem to have been called upon to write any music especially for the joint coronation on 11 April, though his name was on the list of those musicians confirmed in their posts in the Private Musick and scheduled to take part, which was issued a week earlier. It is possible, though unlikely given his royal and Abbey appointments, that nothing fresh was required and that as the chronicler Narcissus Luttrell reported, the ceremony was much as before. This is made even more doubtful because we know that although one of the anthems John Blow (who was by then Organist of St Paul's Cathedral and had no connection with Westminster Abbey) had written for James's coronation, *Behold, O God, Our Defender,* was adapted for William and Mary he was also commissioned to supply two others, *Let My Prayer Come Up* and *The Lord God Is a Sun and Shield.* The ceremony was something of a take-over by St Paul's since it was the Bishop of London, assisted by the Archbishop of York, who officiated. The Archbishop of Canterbury was one of four bishops, including the ubiquitous Bishop Ken of Bath and Wells, who felt that while they could accept the new government, they could not renounce the oaths they had taken at James's coronation such a short time before. Given such a lead there were many loyal Church of England Royalists who took the same position. Parliament had, after all, only voted to crown William and Mary instead of making them Regents – removing the government from James but not the Crown – by three votes. There was disquiet too that accepting William also meant accepting toleration of nonconformists because, though he was pragmatic enough to participate in Anglican rites to gain the throne, William himself was a Calvinist.

Altogether the coronation turned out to be more trouble than it was worth for Purcell, involving him in an acrimonious row with the Dean and Chapter of the Abbey. It had been the practice at previous coronations for the Organist to sell tickets for seats in the organ loft, one of the best vantage points in the Abbey. On this occasion, however, the authorities decided three weeks before the service to call in the money for distribution among all the Abbey staff. Purcell ignored the order, however, and was threatened with the sack a week after the ceremony unless he obeyed. He returned over £78, minus his fee and expenses. Given the low level of Abbey salaries he might have done better to leave the job and keep the money, though the Dean may have been his landlord, which could have proved awkward.

March 25" 1689

It is Order'd that all such Money as shall be raised for Seates at the Coronation within the Church Organ Loft or Church yard shall be paid into the hands of the Treasurer & distributed as the Dean & Chapter shall think fit. And that all vacant Places both in the Church and Church yard which are not taken up & imployed for the Kings use be disposed of by the Dean & Chapter of Westm as they shall think fit.

Aprill: 18: 1689

It is Ordered That Mr Purcell the Organist to ye Dean and Chapter of Westm do pay to the hands of Mr John Needham Receiver of the College All such Money as was received by him for places in the Organ Loft at ye Coronation of King William and Queen Mary on or before Saturday next being ye 20 day of this instant Aprill. And in Defaull thereof his place is declared to be null & void. And It is further Order'd that his Stipend or Salary due at our Lady day last past be detayned in the hands of the Treasurer untill further Order—

The Minutes of the Dean and Chapter of Westminster Abbey recording the demand that Purcell return the proceeds of the entry fee to spectators in the organ loft at the Coronation of William and Mary.

There is a possibility that until Purcell was named in the list of court musicians in early April his position and his prospects under the new regime were far from clear. At a time when suspicion of disloyalty was often as good as proof, Henry, Daniel and Edward Purcell may have found their delicate balancing act becoming uncomfortable. Edward, who had left the royal household for the army on the death of King Charles, had remained loyal to James when his regiment was purged the previous autumn and had been promoted to the rank of Captain. It seems that he was in no hurry to swear an oath of allegiance to the new order. Daniel had been appointed to his post at Magdalen College less than a year before by the now disgraced Bishop Gifford. Meanwhile King James, an experienced and respected General, had recovered the will to keep the throne, which he had so sensibly lost in December, and had landed in Ireland where, in the early months of 1689, he was showing signs of winning. For many of those in London with Irish connections, like Nahum Tate, it was an anxious time. In these circumstances it is quite possible that if Tate did write the libretto for *Dido and Aeneas* in the early autumn of 1688, when rumours of an invitation to William first began to circulate, the 'unfortunate' reading of the story's allegory was precisely the one he intended: while James's daughter Mary was acceptable as Queen, joint rule with a foreigner could only lead to disaster. By the time *Dido* was performed the final outcome of the revolution would still not have been clear. The conciliatory Prologue and Epilogue (the latter written by D'Urfey) that were provided would have obscured the true intent (as would have all the dances). It is interesting though that one of the major parts in the prologue should have been taken by Lady Dorothy Burke, daughter of the Earl of Clanrickarde. He was one of many members of the Anglo-Irish aristocracy who remained loyal to James and was prepared to fight William's invasion of Ireland.

It may be significant that none of the three Purcell brothers gained any new preferment under William. If they were anxious it is hardly surprising. The Purcell family had for two generations forged its position out of unswerving faithfulness to the Stuarts of four, possibly five reigns (depending on whether Thomas and the elder Henry had sung in the choir at Windsor as boys for James I). While increasingly identified with the Anglican cause they had sufficient Catholic connections to bring them under scrutiny whenever there were questions being asked. Purcell may not have known that he still had an official job until the confirmation in the first week of April. The composers' posts, however, seem to have lapsed and were not reinstated by William until 1699 when John Blow was given one of the jobs back.

If this is the case, and if Purcell's first allegiance was to Mary rather than William, it makes sense of the fact that he did not contribute a new work to the coronation but waited another three weeks for the Queen's twenty-seventh birthday on 30 April. For that he wrote the first of his extraordinary series of odes for her, *Now Does The Glorious Day Appear.* The words, by Thomas Shadwell – just named as Poet Laureate in place of his most bitter enemy, John Dryden – clearly uses the occasion when attention was naturally on Mary rather than William to make it clear which of the two monarchs inspired more than token affection:

> 'Our dear religion, with our law's defence,
> To God her zeal, to man benevolence;
> Must her above all former monarchs raise
> To be the everlasting theme of praise.
> No more shall we the great Eliza boast,
> For her great name in greater Mary's will be lost.'

Mary II (1662-1694), a more enthusiastic patron of music and theatre than her husband.

107

William was allowed a somewhat grudging tribute in the previous verse which suggests that his usefulness was strictly as her consort in vanquishing Catholicism:

'Her hero too, whose conduct and whose arms
The trembling Papal world their force must yield
Must bend himself to her victorious charms
And give up all the trophies of the field.'

Even if the queen was present at *Dido's* first performance a few weeks later she does not seem to have taken any offence. If she had it was more likely to have been directed in those days at Tate, the writer, than at Purcell, the mere composer, who by the autumn had been confirmed in his old court appointments. Nonetheless if they had hoped that the work would transfer to the theatre they were to be disappointed, which may indicate that it was controversial. It was not staged professionally until 1700, and then only as a series of masques interpolated into Charles Gildon's rewrite of *Measure for Measure*, by which time Mary and Purcell were long dead, William was secure and Tate had been Poet Laureate for eight years. Only once William himself was dead was *Dido and Aeneas* presented in its own right, fifteen years after its première and shorn of most of its dances.

The manuscript of the ode for Mr. Maidwell's School in Purcell's fair copy book.

The original performance inspired D'Urfey to more than the Epilogue. He had lodged at the school for a while and the next year he came up with his comedy *Love for Money*, or *The Boarding School*, which exploited all the double entendres latent in the subject of nubile girls on the fringe of the adult world. It could have given offence but seems merely to have started a string of in-jokes among the theatrical poets. The opera was followed by Purcell's third commission from a school within a year. Just across the road from Westminster Abbey, in King Street close to where the Chapel Royal boys had their lodging, was a school run by Louis Maidwell. This was a boy's school so no dances were needed from Purcell. Instead, one of the scholars – we have no record of which – wrote the words for an ode, *Celestial Music Did the Gods Inspire* and it was duly performed on 5 August. A month later, on 6 September, the Purcell's latest child was christened Edward in Westminster Abbey. Young Frances was now more than one year old and once again the baby proved strong enough to survive. Although Edward Purcell never achieved as much as his father he was accomplished enough as a musician to be Organist of St Margaret's, Westminster from 1726 until 1740.

Thomas D'Urfey
(1653-1723), close
collaborator of Purcell and
one of his wittiest librettists.

For the second year running Purcell was not required to
write a welcome song in 1689, though John Blow continued to
produce his series of New Year odes. It seemed that the practice
of marking the sovereign's return to the political cockpit of
Whitehall had died with the revolution. Matters were too
insecure, with Ireland by now firmly in James's control, for
celebrations. The reality of William's character was also
making itself felt. He was not the King for the frivolities of
Newmarket or lazy days by the river. He was a dour campaigner
with war in Ireland and the constant threat of war with France
to oversee. As well as a settlement in Scotland (which was
slower in coming and even less wholehearted than it had been
south of the border) and the demands of factious and suspicious
England he had somehow to keep the balance between the
disparate groups in Holland, where he had to exert authority
without stimulating a renewal of republicanism.

Unlike his Stuart relations William was little interested in music away from the parade ground. If he had a preference it was for the martial instruments – oboes, trumpets and drums – which begin to surface in Purcell's music with increasing frequency after 1689. To an extent this was a response to a general trend in European music but it was also a matter of facing up to the new conditions at court. The days when the King would tap his foot to string orchestras in the anthems at the Chapel Royal were over. For one thing the size of the musical establishment itself had now been cut, a move that had been started by James and was continued by William (with further cuts to come the following year). For another the King was rarely in residence. If Catholicism had kept James at the other end of Whitehall Palace, the Thames kept William away altogether. Its damp city airs played havoc with his asthma and he soon looked for alternative accommodation in winter at Holland House, Kensington and in summer at Hampton Court. Whitehall Palace, with its Government bustle, became the centre of royal life only when William was away and Mary was left in sole charge of the kingdom. It was another factor which must have reinforced Purcell's natural leaning to the Queen rather than her distant partner.

With no welcome song to produce and little incentive to make an effort, Purcell seems only to have written one piece for the court in late 1689; a verse anthem, *Praise the Lord O Jerusalem*, for the end of November. For a long time this was thought to be the missing coronation anthem from earlier in the year but, as Robert King points out, the text is for the Sunday before Advent, although it also forms last part of the verses for *My Heart Is Inditing*, one of the regular coronation texts. Its gentle string opening, modest length and rather sombre tone certainly suit a dull November morning in Chapel rather than celebrations in the Abbey.

If the intention behind writing *Dido and Aeneas* had been to re-establish his reputation as a composer for the theatre it undoubtedly worked. That autumn he contributed a song to the difficult tragedy *The Massacre of Paris* – thoroughly controversial when it had been written in 1681, less so with a new King for whom war with France was almost a way of life – by Nathaniel Lee, recently out of Bedlam having spent most of the previous reign there. Purcell eventually found his own setting of the song, 'Thy Genius, Lo!', less than satisfactory and reset it for the 1695 revival. Betterton, however, was by this time more

Nathaniel Lee (1653-1692), the brilliant but mentally unstable writer for several of whose plays Purcell wrote the incidental music.

convinced of Purcell's worth. Admittedly the removal of the foreign composers meant that he had fewer recognised talents to turn to. However he was confident enough to employ Purcell for the most ambitious score since the disastrous *Albion and Albanius* five years earlier.

Dioclesian, or *The Prophetess* was adapted by Betterton from a play of the same name (though the title and the sub-title were reversed in the original) by Philip Massinger and John Fletcher, which had first been produced in 1622. The main theme was the folly of dividing kingdoms, a popular one in the reign of James VI and I. Its revival, at a time when the monarchy was much less secure and when Scotland was having second thoughts about the union of its Crown with England, shows the disaffection many of the artists of the time must have felt as their patronage from the court diminished. If *Albion and Albanius* was a paean to the triumph of Charles II's version of monarchy, *Dioclesian,* with its story of an ineffectual emperor and his equally useless successors, was an essay in disillusion. Betterton's careful alterations of the original writers' text emphasised the parallels with recent experience. Dryden, who had so confidently backed the wrong horse five years earlier, shared in the bitterness and provided a prologue to the work, which was promptly banned by the Lord Chamberlain for the second performance.

In the 1620s productions of *The Prophetess* there was space for plenty of music (though it is unclear who wrote it) but Purcell introduced a great deal more, in particular the 40-minute Masque that was added on to the action at the end. The Masque offered Purcell another opportunity to collaborate with Josias Priest and it continued to stand on its own as a concert piece long after the rest of the play was out of fashion. Unlike his previous theatre music and reflecting the new orchestral arrangements (and in the light of the increased reliance on musicians outside the court) Purcell includes extensive parts for trumpets and oboes in the forces for *Dioclesian.* The change is abrupt, coming suddenly in 1690 throughout his music and, having barely used any instruments other than strings (whether bowed or plucked) until then, Purcell used the larger orchestra for almost all his major works from then on. This must reflect that, for the first time, they were at his disposal. Either there was a change in the job descriptions of the royal wind and brass players or those commissioning Purcell could afford more generous fees for the players.

That was certainly the case for his next work, an Ode with words by D'Urfey for the annual dinner of Yorkshire gentlemen, held at Merchant Taylor's Hall in the City on 27 March 1690. They were prepared to spend £100 on its performance and Purcell obliged with resplendent trumpet fanfares and orchestral symphonies. Held just after the elections for a new Parliament, which had forced the postponement of the feast for a month, the event took the opportunity to celebrate the first year of the new reign. D'Urfey's verses took care to compare York (given its old Roman name of Brigantium) favourably with London's 'puny town' and extol the Yorkshiremen's part in James's overthrow:

And now when the renown'd Nassau
Came to restore our liberty and law,
The work so well perform'd and done,
They were the first, the first begun.

They did no storms nor threatnings fear
Of thunder in the grumbling air,
Or any revolutions near.

Tom D'Urfey was the author of the words for the second commission of the spring, *Arise, My Muse*, the Queen's Birthday Ode for 30 April. It is freer in its verse than most of the occasional pieces of the time and consequently one of the best texts that Purcell was given to set. The more grandiose tastes of the younger generation of Stuarts are immediately clear from the instrumentation. Instead of the gentle string ritornellos of the old welcome songs there are stately processions of oboes and trumpets. Because natural trumpets without valves were not as nimble to play and did not have as many notes as their modern successors, the writing was inevitably more limited harmonically and slower paced than in the works that used only strings but it was more immediately impressive. *Arise My Muse* veers between the simple glorification that appealed to William's military nature and the lilting poignancy that characterised Purcell's affectionate writing for Mary.

William was about to embark for Ireland where, despite the lifting of the Siege of Londonderry, James still held out a year and a half after his less than glorious flight from London. William must have been regretting his reasonableness in letting him escape. In retrospect it would perhaps have been better if William had allowed James to keep Ireland in return

William III leads his troops against his father-in-law at the Battle of the Boyne near Drogheda, 11 July 1690.

for a formal abdication in England and Scotland. That, though, was beyond the vision of the moment and was anyway made impossible by the fact that both William and Louis XIV were using the battle for Ireland as a proxy war to settle the real issue between the liberal Dutch Stadholder and the autocratic French emperor; the direction of European monarchy. With Holland, England and Scotland in his grasp William was a much more formidable opponent for Louis than he had been in the past. For the first time since the Restoration the king in England could not be kept under control either by religious affinity or secret payment. The last thing on anybody's mind was the cause of Irish independence or the future peace of the two islands.

William left for Ireland in the first weeks of June 1690 just as *Dioclesian* was opening. The opera was an immediate and immense success, justifying Betterton's gamble in mounting the most extensive piece of music-theatre with an English composer since Matthew Locke's death 14 years before. Dryden's prologue expressed the company's worry about the costs and, in the guise of a lament about the absence of male members of the audience, attacked the Irish campaign, which was why it was banned.

> A play which like a Prospective set right,
> Presents our vast Expences close to sight;
> But turn the Tube, and there we sadly view
> Our distant gains; and those uncertain too.
> A sweeping Tax, which on our selves we raise;
> And all like you, in hopes of better days....
> New Honour calls you hence; and all your Care
> Is to provide the horrid pomp of War:
> In Plume and Scarf, Jack-boots and Bilbo Blade
> Your Silver goes, that should support our Trade.

Purcell's music was an important ingredient in *Dioclesian's* success but it was not the only one. His splendid Masque music was the accompaniment to a stage set which surpassed anything seen in London for 15 years. An extract from the stage directions gives an idea of its splendour:

'While a symphony is playing, a machine descends, so large it fills all the space from the frontispiece of the stage to the further end of the house, and fixes itself by two ladders to the floor. In it are four several stages, representing the Palaces of two Gods and two Goddesses. ...The whole object is terminated with a glowing cloud on which a chair of state, all of gold, the Sun breaking through the cloud, and making a glory about it; as this descends there rises from under the stage a pleasant prospect of a noble garden, consisting of fountains, and orange trees set in large vases; the middle walk leads to a Palace at a great distance. ... The Dancers place themselves on every stage in the machine; the Singers range themselves about the stage.'

It is a production which would be hard for theatres today to match, technically or financially. Had it failed it could have ruined Betterton at a time when subsidy from the court was less forthcoming it had been ten years before. Without his monopoly of theatrical presentation it is very doubtful whether he would have been able to sustain such extravagance.

Dryden was impressed too, as he admitted in his preface to his new comedy, *Amphitryon,* or *The Two Sosias,* produced a little later in the year (Queen Mary went to see it in late October at about the same time as the play was published). It had been a difficult time for Dryden, now nearly 60, who now found himself with the wrong religion and deprived of his public office 'to the ruin of my small fortune' as he admitted. This threw him back on the theatre and translation as ways of making a living and, in the light of his experience over the preceding years, this cannot have been easy. With the general clear-out of the Italian and French composers, whom he had long thought better than anybody native to London, he was forced to look to English musicians. In 1685, when he had most forcibly expressed the opinion, it cannot be said to have been too unfair, given the fact that Purcell was unproven in the theatre, Blow was not very successfully pursuing his own operatic path and Locke and Humfrey were dead. Simon Pack, William Turner and Thomas Farmer were not in the same class. By 1690 Dryden had no alternative, although there were up-and-coming figures like John Eccles and Godfrey Finger emerging, and *Dioclesian* changed his mind about Purcell:

'What has been wanting on my Part has been abundantly supplied by the Excellent Composition of Mr. Purcell; in whose Person we have at length found an English Man, equal with the best abroad. At least my opinion of him has been such, since his happy and judicious Performances in the late Opera; and the Experience I have had of him, in the setting of my three Songs for this Amphitryon: To all of which, and particularly to the Composition of the Pastoral Dialogue, the numerous Quire of Fair Ladies gave so just an Applause on the Third Day.'

Purcell not only set the three songs, he also provided the overture and several dances, amounting to over half an hour of music. The somewhat chastened Dryden, reduced to stating in print his obedience to the government, was stressing the success of the third performance because by tradition that was the author's benefit, so Purcell's popularity was putting money in Dryden's pocket at a moment when he desperately needed it.

By the autumn of 1690, after years of neglect, Purcell was writing almost full time for the theatre. On the 9 September, just after his son Edward's first birthday, he completed an anthem for the Chapel Royal, *My Song Shall Be Alway of the Loving Kindness of the Lord,* but it was his only one for the year. He seems not to have written anything for the important royal occasions after April; the birth of a son to Princess Anne, the return of William from his victorious Irish campaign in September or the King's birthday in November. Instead he wrote eight short dances for *Distressed Innocence* or *The Princess of Persia,* by Elkanah Settle and William Mountfort, which was also performed that October. It was an extraordinary month for the public exposure of Purcell's music. It also saw the première of Thomas Southerne's first comedy *Sir Anthony Love,* or *The Rambling Lady,* designed as a vehicle for Mountfort's comedienne wife, Susanna, who made a speciality of trouser roles. For this Purcell wrote an overture and three songs. This too was an immediate success, launching Southerne as one of the most entertaining and popular playwrights of the time. It meant that at the opening of the season in Dorset Gardens and Drury Lane Purcell had four productions including an opera running in repertoire at the same time. The musicians of the orchestra could have been forgiven for wanting a chance to play something else. At the same time as the music was being heard in the theatre it was appearing in print. There were catches, songs and duets in the latest volumes of *The Banquet of Music* and eight new pieces in the new edition of the rival *Apollo's Banquet* (not exactly radically different titles for the collections).

In the two years either side of his thirtieth birthday in 1689 Purcell's life had changed out of all recognition. He had been an out-of-favour court composer spending much of his time as an organist, teacher and repairer of instruments, with a marriage that had become a miserable round of pregnancy and death. By the end of 1690 he was the most fêted song-writer in the country, with two thriving children and a position at court that was as secure as any musician's in those uncertain years could have been. His music shows revitalised confidence and

An engaging doodle, possibly a self-portrait, on a manuscript purported to be Purcell's in the Theatre Museum London.

freedom, a new assurance with large forces and a greater gift for operatic structure than any of his contemporaries, which (unlike Locke) he could explore without having to share the commission with others. He was even, in the theatre at least, finding the chance to write the sort of forward looking orchestral music which his colleagues in France were making their own. Purcell brought to that his exciting blend of English melody and Italian virtuosity. It was the beginning of his most impressive period. The glorious day was indeed appearing.

Chapter 7

Universal Applause

Purcell would have been working harder than usual performing for the court in the early months of 1691. In January King William had returned to Holland for the first time since his accession, taking Nicholas Staggins and the majority of the royal instrumentalists with him. While they were away the Queen moved back to Whitehall Palace from Holland House for the winter. Those musicians left behind would have had the Chapel Royal and private entertainments for Queen Mary and Princess Anne to occupy them. With so much of the musical establishment abroad, including some extra freelance players (keeping William's allies amused while they talked about how to deal with France) the theatres were unable to present any plays with substantial amounts of music. The exception for Purcell was *The Gordion Knot Unty'd,* scored for only a small string ensemble. It is unclear who the author of this lost play was and Purcell seems to have been too busy to have composed more than ten minutes worth of dances for it. At least two of the eight movements were lifted from earlier welcome songs, a practice of self-plagiary which Purcell indulged in very rarely. He made sure of the music's topical popularity, though, by using *Lilliburlero* as the bass line of a little jig before a much grander chaconne. By now it was becoming something of a signature tune for him after it had been adopted by William's troops in the fight for Ireland.

There was a considerable amount of irritation involved in the printing of the complete music for *Dioclesian,* which Purcell

Holland House, Kensington, adopted by William and Mary as their London home because William found that the river air at Whitehall was bad for his asthma.

118

embarked on that winter as his second private venture in publishing. He dedicated it to the Duke of Somerset, a close ally of Princess Anne in her brewing row with her sister and brother-in-law, and Dryden wrote a gracious preface. Purcell himself wrote a less effusive note at the end which suggests that he was soon regretting having anything to do with the project. He apologises for the delay – presumably the intention had originally been to publish the score at the same time as Dryden published the libretto the previous October but it was March by the time it was ready for the subscribers – and apologises for the fact that several of the songs had appeared in unauthorised sheets in the meantime;

'...I employed two several Printers; but One of them falling into some trouble, and the Volume swelling to a bulk beyond my expectation, have been the Occasions of this Delay. It has been objected that some of the Songs are already common; but I presume that the Subscribers upon perusal of the Work, will easily be convinc'd that they are not the Essential Parts of it.'

Finally he complains that he miscalculated the eventual costs and that, far from making him the expected profit, 'the Subscription-money will scarcely amount to the Expence of compleating this Edition.'

In the meantime Purcell had a birthday ode to write for April, the third in his sequence for the Queen, and was working with Dryden on a new opera which was even more ambitious musically – though it can hardly have been scenically – than *Dioclesian*. This was *King Arthur*, or the *British Worthy*, which Dryden had first drafted as a sequel to *Albion and Albanius* but had abandoned when that ill-fated work had met with such a poor reception. We can be grateful that he did, otherwise it would have been Grabu, not Purcell, who would have supplied the music and we would have been deprived of some of Purcell's most ingenious settings, including the famous frost scene from act three (the excuse for clever staging) which to a remarkable degree anticipates Vivaldi's concerto depiction of winter 30 years later.

Dryden had to make several alterations to make the story appropriate to the 1690s. In theory the last thing that he wanted to do was to further upset the government. The storyline was unrecognisable from anything out of Malory. Inventing a fantastical combination of Merlin, spirits and elves with an impossible version of the Briton King Arthur's battles against the Saxons, it ended with a satisfactory reconciliation of the two peoples. However, this had more to do with the unification of the crowns of England and Scotland by the Stuarts than peace between Celt and Teuton. In the final chorus Dryden brings William III into the picture with a verse that managed to misrepresent his attitude to Holland completely;

> Our Natives not alone appear
> To court this Martial Prize;
> But Foreign Kings Adopted here
> Their Crowns at home despise.

Since William had only been back in London for three weeks before Louis XIV's siege of Mons had forced him to return to Holland – at dawn on 1 May, after Mary's birthday celebrations including Purcell's *Welcome, Welcome, Glorious Morn* the previous day – and was beginning to make it plain that of his four nations he infinitely preferred his Dutch one, Dryden's quatrain can only have been either ignorant or satirical. The latter is much the most likely, given his – and probably Purcell's – discomfort with William's regime.

King Arthur followed the pattern of *Dioclesian* the year before, being premièred in late May or early June and continuing in the repertoire through the autumn. As with earlier operas, apart from *Albion, Dido* and *Venus and Adonis,* Dryden and Purcell stuck to the English practice of saving the music for commentary on the plot and special scenes of magic or rustic celebration. The main characters did not sing nor was the main action set to music as it would have been in an Italian or French opera. The aim was for the speaking parts to remain as naturalistic as possible while providing plenty of opportunity for spectacle that heightened the excitement of the story. On the London stage music was a vital part of any production but the belief then was that audiences could not be expected to suspend their disbelief in scenes which did not bear some relation to the moment when characters would, or would not, sing in real life. So choruses might be sung in the fields or as part of a ceremony. Love songs were sung to illustrate the protagonists' emotions, rather than sung to the beloved, and dances which were a natural consequence of the scene (in an age much more given to social dancing than ours) were considered appropriate. The rest was left to normal dramatic dialogue. In this the London operas – or semi-operas as they clumsily now tend to be called – differed both from the opera as it developed in the rest of Europe and from the modern musical which allows singing in circumstances which then would have been considered absurd and which still are by many who feel uncomfortable with opera's conventions. As Peter Motteux, who might be described as London's first arts journalist, put it in the launching edition of *The Gentleman's Journal* in January 1692,

'Other nations bestow the name of Opera only on such Plays whereof every word is sung. But experience hath taught us that our English genius will not rellish that perpetual Singing.'

Sadly, because we have also lost the framework of classical mythological allusion which was at the heart of all serious baroque theatre (and which anybody with an education would then have understood as naturally as we do the characters in *Superman, Star Trek* or *James Bond*), we cannot enjoy pieces like *King Arthur* and *Dioclesian* with anything like the immediacy that contemporary audiences could. This does not make them ridiculous. It only shows that theatre based on convention has an almost impossible barrier to surmount when those conventions are no longer recognised. At the time *King Arthur* was considered one of the best things that had been done on the London stage since the Restoration. It re-established Dryden's reputation at a time when it been severely mauled and it made Purcell unassailable as the leading English composer of the age, indeed of the century. Nobody else had ever reached out to such a large section of the population with his songs (like 'What Shall I Do' from *Dioclesian* which was popular enough for Gay and Pepusch to include it in *The Beggar's Opera* forty years later) or commanded the same measure of admiration at court, in the church or – increasingly – abroad.

Towards the end of 1691 Thomas Southerne returned to Purcell for incidental music to his second comedy, *The Wives' Excuse*, or *Cuckolds Make Themselves*. This inventive play, which was

King Arthur, the 1995 tercentenary production directed by Graham Vick at the Théatre du Châtelet in Paris and the Royal Opera House, Covent Garden.

revived only in 1995, was perhaps the first to depict a concert; a typical music meeting of the time with the servants forced to wait outside and the gentlemen within clamouring to have their attempts at composition sung. Purcell, who after all his experience at writing catches was as good at producing satirical music as serious stuff, had the fun of parodying the songwriting of the amateurs who were not quite as gifted as they thought. Just how accurate Southerne and Purcell were, in the lyrics sung by Charlotte Butler and Will Mountfort, can be gauged from the distinctly unamused reaction to the spoof concert from those who thought their honest pleasures were being sent up; which they were. Southerne felt stung into defending his picture of the music meeting when the play was published the following year. 'I introduc'd it, as a fashionable Scene of bringing good Company together, without a Design of abusing what every Body likes...'

Thomas Southerne (1660-1746), whose play *The Wives's Excuse* was the first to satirise public concerts. It was revived with Purcell's music for the first time since 1691 by the Royal Shakespeare Company in 1995.

For the next two years *The Gentleman's Journal* proved to be a useful outlet for Purcell, publishing several of his songs and giving generous coverage to his theatre music. It was a remarkable publication, the inspiration of its 19-year-old editor, Peter Motteux, a French Protestant who had been forced by the persecution that followed the repeal of the Edict of Nantes in 1685 to flee his native Rouen when he was 12. *The Gentleman's Journal* was the nearest equivalent to what we would now see as a monthly magazine and a refreshing alternative to the official government-sponsored news sheet, *The London Gazette*. Although Motteux was forced by inadequate finances to close the *Journal* after only two years, it paved the way for Addison and Steele's longer lasting ventures, *The Tatler* and *The Spectator,* in the first decades of the next century.

As Motteux mentioned in the first issue of the *Journal, King Arthur* was still running in December but Purcell was already at work on the extravaganza for the following spring, a adaptation of Shakespeare's *A Midsummer Night's Dream* (which had hardly been performed at all in London since Killigrew's day) to be called *The Fairy-Queen*. He was lucky to have a theatre to write for since a brawl at a performance just before Christmas had led to a complaint being referred to the House of Lords which initially closed performances, though the ban was relaxed on appeal.

We do not know who was responsible for recasting Shakespeare's original play. The adaptation has come in for some hysterical criticism over the years which has more to do with the cult of the Bard than the shortcomings of the 1692 production. The suggestion of Elkanah Settle seems unlikely. The subject matter would have suited Tom D'Urfey's mischievous wit but the writing for the sections set by Purcell is really not good enough to have been by him, even if he had not been trying very hard, and if he was meant to be seen in the character of the drunk poet it would probably have been too much to ask that he should have satirised himself, though this could be a later interpolation, perhaps by Southerne. The libretto is comparable to that for *Dioclesian* and it makes sense that if that was by Betterton, so was *The Fairy-Queen*. Betterton had after all been involved in presenting new versions of Shakespeare for over 30 years and, even if it is not to modern tastes, which prefer more authentic treatments, the handling of cuts and alterations to make room for Purcell's semi-opera is clever. It is also clear that, while he was interested in the opera as a musical spectacle, Betterton had no intention of planning far enough ahead to commission completely new texts. *Dioclesian* had been a good property as *The Prophetess* for many years, Dryden's *King Arthur* was already on the stocks though unproduced and *A Midsummer's Night's Dream* was due for a revival. Most importantly, the separation between the real and the fairy court in the story (which is made to vanish at the end of *The Fairy-Queen* though it is reinforced earlier) offered an obvious way to develop masques that could build on the expectations of the opera audience for spectacular scenery. The antics of Shakespeare's mechanicals (Bottom and co.; the equivalent of the anti-masque characters in Ben Jonson's entertainments for the Jacobean court) also gave Purcell a chance to return to the rustic buffoonery that had proved so popular in *King Arthur.* Then as now there is nothing the urban sophisticates of London like to laugh at more than a few yokels. Purcell makes the parallel worlds of Thesius's Athens and Oberon's kingdom into a baroque fantasy of masques and transformations. Modern presentations of *The Fairy-Queen* tend to do away with the spoken drama and concentrate on Purcell's music. This is surely doing even more damage to the conception of the semi-opera than it did to Shakespeare. It reflects the inflexibility of late twentieth-century theatre, divided between opera companies and straight playhouses in a way that would have seemed ridiculous in the 1690s.

Even though Purcell was only setting parts of what appeared on stage, this still amounts to two hours of music (a few minutes of which were added the following season). It represents by far his longest work. However he still managed to write other things at the same time. There was his usual Birthday Ode for the Queen at the end of April, *Love's Goddess Sure Was Blind,* which was written for the occasion by Sir Charles Sedley, not only a courtier of the old school but a fine Restoration playwright whose last play in 1687 had been called *Bellamira, or The Mistress;* an appropriate title since he was also the father of James's mistress, Catherine. Whatever his daughter's affections, however, Sedley himself was a firm and proven supporter of the new regime. Considering that *The Fairy-Queen* was in its final rehearsals it is hardly surprising that the Ode was not one of Purcell's more magnificent. It reverted to his old habit of using an accompanying orchestra of strings without oboes and trumpets, a decision which may also have been eased because William, who preferred the more ceremonial sound, was away campaigning in the Low Countries. Its intimacy was enhanced by his allusion to an in-joke between him and the Queen. Earlier in the year she had asked Purcell, John Gostling and Arabella Hunt (Princess Anne's music teacher) to perform for her. After a while and, the story implies, rather a lot of Purcell, the Queen asked Arabella Hunt to sing a Scottish ballad instead, accompanying herself on the lute. Its title, 'Cold and Raw,' seems to have described neatly how Purcell felt at being left with nothing to do. He made the point graciously by using the tune as the base line for one of the movements of *Love's Goddess Sure Was Blind.*

The Queen was responsible for complicating the preparations for *The Fairy-Queen* still further when she banned Dryden's new tragedy *Cleomenes,* which had one song by Purcell, for being critical of her government. The opera's première was then moved forward to fill the gap which may account for the fact that some numbers, including one of the funniest – the scene for the drunken poet, Sutter – were not included until the following year. In the event *Cleomenes* was allowed to take the stage two weeks before the Queen's birthday (causing no further problems for Dryden) and the opening of *The Fairy-Queen* was moved back once again, though only by four days, to 2 May.

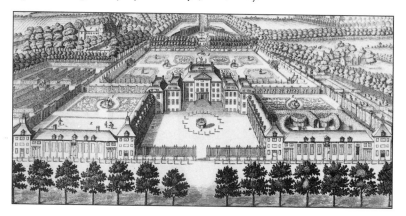

Het Loo, near Apeldoorn, Holland, which William and Mary made their Dutch home in 1686.

By the time it was produced Betterton was having second thoughts about the profitability of the new-found enthusiasm for opera. Despite the public acclaim he could not recoup the amount needed if the expectations for music and spectacle were to be met. The costs of the scenery, costumes and music came to £3,000, an astonishing amount for a theatre that, as the preface to *The Fairy-Queen* complained, received nothing like the subsidies of comparable royal houses on the continent. It is depressing but inevitable given the continuity of Tory attitudes over the centuries that Betterton's appeal in 1692 reads remarkably like that of the Director of the Royal Opera House, Covent Garden three hundred years later. *The Fairy-Queen's* author argued that if London had a properly supported opera house it would bring great benefits to the city and that if English productions were given half the backing they were in France, the dancers would be as good as there – almost exactly the position today. Half the amount is still galling. Comparing London unfavourably with Paris was likely to prove even less effective in 1692 than it is now, however, especially during a summer which saw William lose the Siege of Namur and a string of engagements to French forces. British regiments had been fighting for the Dutch in the low countries for a century but it cannot have made their increased commitment by William in his perpetual trial of strength with Louis any easier to stomach, even when anti-French feeling was constantly whipped up by rumours of invasion.

After the experience with *Dioclesian*, Purcell did not want to see his work appear again in editions which would bring him no reward and had some of the numbers printed himself by Heptinstall. These were sold at Dorset Gardens and the shops owned by John Carr and Henry Playford near the Temple. He did not go so far as to issue the full score, however – he had learned that expensive lesson from the *Dioclesian* saga too. This proved disastrous for *The Fairy-Queen's* subsequent performance history because the score was lost after his death. Despite a desperate appeal made in October 1700 by the Treasurer of the theatre, Zachary Biggs, for its return (with a reward of 20 guineas offered) it disappeared until the end of the nineteenth century, when a copy was found in the library of the Royal Academy of Music (which had not been established as a conservatory until 1822).

For the rest of the season Purcell was represented in the theatre almost by guest appearances, contributing a song but rarely more to several plays; D'Urfey's *The Marriage-Hater*

John Dryden (1631-1700),
the most distinguished poet
and playwright of the
Restoration age.

Match'd, John Crowne's *Regulus* (which opened a few weeks after *The Fairy-Queen*) and a revival of Dryden's *Aureng-Zebe,* a verse tragedy set in India and originally staged 17 years earlier. Another Dryden revival which may also have come from 1692, the version of *Oedipus* he wrote with Nathaniel Lee, contains what is now Purcell's best-loved song, 'Music For a While.' It is also possible that he wrote his score for Shadwell's *The Libertine* that year. The play was republished then and Shadwell himself died. Since *The Libertine,* his version of the Don Juan story, was his most popular work it would have been a fitting tribute. It includes another of Purcell's more enduring pieces, though quite why it became so ubiquitous I have never been able to understand. Had the Victorian worthies who adopted 'Nymphs and Shepherds Come Away' for so many young ladies' choirs taken the trouble to read the play in which it came they would probably have run a mile. The Libertine is a far more violent and explicit piece than Da Ponte's *Don Giovanni.* 'Nymphs and Shepherds' serves much the same purpose in the stage version as the duet' 'La ci darem la mano in Mozart's score.'

For the moment at the end of the story when Don Juan is dragged down to hell Purcell wrote the solemn trumpet dirge which he used two years later for the music heard at Queen Mary's funeral. This has caused a certain amount of confusion because in retrospect it seems so insensitive to have used the music from such a lurid work for such a solemn occasion. Some biographers have argued that the play was not staged until the summer or autumn of 1694, after the Queen's funeral. But given the emotional climate surrounding the mourning for her, that would surely have made the music's connection with *The Libertine* even more blatant. The 1692 date at least means that less attentive members of the audience would have had time to forget the tune.

It was only nine years since Purcell had first written an ode for the celebrations organised by the gentlemen of the Musical Society but the changes in that time must have made it seem a great deal longer. Perhaps as a result of hearing *The Yorkshire Feast Ode* the Society turned again to Purcell in 1692. This time there was nothing to be composed for the court that autumn to divide his energies as there had been in 1683 when *Welcome To All the Pleasures* had had to share working time with *Fly, Bold Rebellion.* Neither was he constrained to rely on the reduced number of musicians available in the King's employ. The St Cecilia's Day feast in Stationers' Hall was now an elaborate affair for which composers produced their grandest works. In 1692 Purcell did just that, writing an ode of impressive proportions which surpassed anything he had done in the form before. For a text he turned to Nicholas Brady, a close collaborator of Nahum Tate, with whom Brady was working on a metrical version of the Psalms which retained its popularity throughout the nineteenth century. He was also the vicar of St Catherine Cree, the church where Purcell and Blow had judged the new organ and organist five years before. Brady obliged with *Hail, Bright Cecilia* and Purcell fashioned it into a work of 13 movements, including one of his longest orchestral symphonies. Motteux in *The Gentleman's Journal* was full of praise, reporting how the Ode

'was admirably set to Music by Mr. Henry Purcell, and performed twice with universal applause, particularly the second stanza, which was sung with incredible graces by Mr. Purcell himself. Though I was enjoined not to name the author of the Ode, I find a great reluctance to forbear letting you know whom you must thank for so beautiful a poem.'

Motteux could plainly not contain himself because the next month he went as far as naming 'Mr. B-y' as the writer. Robert King has argued that Purcell did not actually sing the counter-tenor solo, 'Tis Nature's Voice' and that Motteux merely meant that he had supplied the vocal graces. W.H. Cummings, though, refers to an early edition of the song from Purcell's lifetime which reiterates that he sang it himself and, given his long career at the Chapel Royal there is no reason whatever why he should not have done. He may not have sung at every performance though, which would explain the reference on one score to John Pate, who had also sung counter-tenor in *The Fairy-Queen*. We know from *The London Gazette* that it was revived at the end of January 1694

'at the Consort-Room in York-Buildings, on this present Thursday, at the usual hour... together with some other Compositions of his, both Vocal and Instrumental, for the Entertainment of His Highness Prince Lewis of Baden.'

Earlier in November William Mountfort appeared in *Henry the Second, King of England,* with Anne Bracegirdle, who had succeeded Nell Gwynne in the public's esteem as favourite actress. She played Rosamund, his unwilling mistress, for whom is sung a song of Purcell's, 'In Vain 'Gainst Love I Strove.' This song came to have poignant memories for all the company. Anne Bracegirdle may have been as young as 18. However she already

Anne Bracegirdle
(1674?-1748), the most
popular actress of the
1690s whose love life
became a constant source
of fascination for the
public of the time.

had a reputation as a woman of unassailable virtue, the characteristic of many of the parts she played. It does seem that she was genuinely uninterested in becoming the mistress of anybody at court or in being linked with any other member of the company. For her admirers this merely added to her allure. Dryden wrote several play epilogues for her in which she teased and rebuffed potential suitors. Congreve was in love with her for years without lasting success, though they spent a great deal of time in each other's company and he was devastated when she married someone else. The composer John Eccles wrote most of his theatre songs for her (sadly this association meant that she does not seem to have sung Purcell's).

In December that year, 1692, her reputation and Mountfort's defence of it led directly to his death. He was the victim of two upper-class teenage tearaways, Lord Mohun and Captain Richard Hill. As was quite usual in theatrical life Hill made advances to her after performances and demanded that she marry him. Anne Bracegirdle refused to have anything to do with him, so Hill and Mohun planned a kidnap attempt, employing six soldiers to seize her outside the house where she was dining. She, together with her mother and Frances Knight, a fellow actress, fought them off and Hill and Mohun then either accompanied or followed her home, depending on whose version was to be believed. There were rumours that Mountfort was Anne Bracegirdle's lover, though he was married to one of the other stars of the company, Susanna Percival. It was his bad luck that he was on his way to Anne Bracegirdle's house just as Mohun and Hill were finally driven from it shouting about what they would like to do to the actor. When Mountfort appeared Mohun challenged him and the 28-year-old Mountfort, no doubt thinking that he could deal with a couple of drunken youths, told Hill what he thought of him. Hill promptly drew his sword and killed Mountfort in the street.

His death robbed the theatre of a talented playwright, one of Betterton's best leading men, and one of the few with a voice good enough to do justice to Purcell's songs, many of which had been written for him. Purcell played the organ at his funeral in St Clement Danes on 13 December. The theatre community was shaken. In the same season it lost two other leading actors, Anthony Leigh and James Nokes. Charlotte Butler, one of the most accomplished singers of Purcell's theatre songs, defected to the emerging theatre in Dublin. Anne Bracegirdle refused to return to the stage until after Mohun's trial for murder by the

House of Lords at the beginning of February (Hill had escaped and died five years later in another fight). To many people's disgust, as John Evelyn noted on 4 February, he was acquitted:

'whether in commiseration of his youth, being not eighteen years old, though exceeding dissolute, or upon whatever other reason, the King himself present some part of the trial, and satisfied, as they report, that he was culpable, sixty-nine acquitted him, only fourteen condemned him.'

On stage the members of the company had a chance to deal with the inferences that had been drawn from the affair when they presented D'Urfey's *The Richmond Heiress: or, A Woman Once In the Right* in April. In this production, Anne Bracegirdle played the role of Fulvia, the eponymous role in which she rejects all her suitors and ends the play refusing to marry. Eccles and Purcell provided the music, with Eccles's contribution being more successful at first (largely because Bracegirdle was singing his mad song and not that by Purcell), though the play itself was not. Dryden reported in a letter to William Walsh that 'it was suffered but foure dayes; and then kickd off for ever'. He described everything but the second act as 'woefull stuff' and took some relish in pointing out that the evening 'concluded with Catcalls'. In fact the play was revived and seems to been greeted more generously once D'Urfey had revised it.

In the intervening months between Mountfort's death and *The Richmond Heiress* in April Purcell's output for the theatre continued unabated. In February three songs of his, including the substantial duet 'No, Resistance Is But Vain,' were included in Southerne's *The Maid's Last Prayer: or, Any Rather Than Fail* which marked the second attack in a row by Southerne of dilettante music evenings. The complaints are led by the splendid Sir Symphony whose feelings at what he is hearing sum up gloriously the experience of a bad concert; 'Captain, you play the wrong Tune – O law! my Teeth! my Teeth! for God's sake, Captain, mind your Cittern'. The last of the three lyrics Purcell set for Southerne's comedy was actually by William Congreve, who like Nahum Tate and Southerne had come from Dublin.

William Congreve (1670-1729). His love for Anne Bracegirdle and defection from Rich to Betterton's company meant that Purcell wrote music for his plays less than he might have done.

Congreve had arrived to pursue his law studies at the Middle Temple in 1689. His first play was produced in March 1693 after encouragement and a fair amount of editing from Dryden, and it launched him immediately into the top rank of playwrights. He was helped by the fact that the title role of *The Old Batchelour* was taken by Betterton himself, with Anne Bracegirdle as the young and pretty Araminta and Mountfort's widow Susanna as her older friend Belinda. Purcell added to the allure with one of his most engaging sets of act tunes and two songs, the first for tenor with the succulent title 'Thus to a Ripe, Consenting Maid' an explanation of how men lose interest once they have satisfied their desire. Perhaps not surprisingly Congreve became the latest frustrated victim of Anne Bracegirdle's charm, and he wasted most of the following decade in love with her. He had better luck with the formidable Henrietta Churchill, later Duchess of Marlborough in her own right, who gave him a daughter in 1723, six years before his death.

In April Purcell turned to the new poet laureate, his old collaborator Nahum Tate, for the Queen's Birthday Ode. Once again King William was away fighting during the celebrations but this time Purcell used the full orchestra available, including some spectacularly difficult writing for solo trumpet. Either he was short of time to compose *Celebrate This Festival*, however, or he felt that the Queen should have had a chance to hear *Hail Bright Cecilia* for he tacked the Overture from six months before onto the new piece. For the first time in three years there was no operatic extravaganza to première in the spring of 1693. Betterton was no longer prepared to take the financial risk. Purcell had to be content for much of the rest of the year with writing a few incidental pieces for an adaptation of Moliere by Thomas Wright, *The Female Virtuosos*, and a revival of Shadwell's best play *Epsom Wells*, staged perhaps as a tribute to the old writer who has unjustly become more famous for his long fight with Dryden than his considerable contribution to the Restoration stage.

After such a frenetic few years Purcell could be forgiven for having a relatively quiet summer and autumn in 1693. It was a worrying time for those connected with the court. William's war with France was proving to be expensive in money and lives. William himself was wounded at the Battle of Landon. When news came that he was safe Mary ordered a period of national thanksgiving, for which Purcell dutifully composed one of his last anthems, *O Give Thanks Unto the Lord.* His songs continued to be published, lighter ones in *The Gentleman's Journal* and the usual anthologies, more substantial ones in the new volume of *Harmonia Sacra.* Purcell contributed five items to this. They went much further than being devotional equivalents of his secular songs. Despite the change of political regime the influence of

Italian composers on his music, which had been gathering force throughout the 1680s, continued. Although he tended to favour English and Irish idioms in his everyday theatre music, in the semi-operas and his other work his admiration for the harmonic discipline and the formal structures of Italian music was growing stronger. London, with its burgeoning concert life, was becoming an important city for touring Italian solo performers, especially singers, who brought the cantatas and arias of Purcell's close contemporary, Alessandro Scarlatti, in their repertoire. Many violin virtuosi travelled to London too and it would have been surprising if Staggins had not included the fashionable string concertos of Corelli in the music performed by the court orchestra, perhaps with Purcell playing the harpsichord continuo. The result of this fascination with Italy was a curious fusion in the *Harmonia Sacra* works, like Tate's *The Blessed Virgin's Expostulation* (these days an almost inevitable audition piece for young sopranos) and *In Guilty Night* between the style of the solo movements from his Chapel Royal anthems and the Italian cantata.

1693 closed well for Purcell. In December Frances again gave birth to a daughter and she was christened Mary (perhaps after the Queen) Peters (her mother's maiden name). In November Congreve's second play (and the first still to be an indispensable part of the repertoire today), *The Double Dealer,* was launched. Purcell wrote a particularly inspiring overture for it, together with several other incidental movements which set the scenes beautifully. There was also a song, 'Cynthia Frowns,' for Mrs. Ayliffe, who with the loss of Charlotte Butler to Dublin, was taking many of Purcell's singing roles. Perhaps as a result of Anne Bracegirdle's refusal to sing music by anybody except John Eccles, Purcell was tending to write songs which suited the specialist singers in the company more than the actors. This has had its effect on modern performances since directors seem loath to have members in the cast who do not take part in the action. But the absurd outcome of this is that, even when great pains are taken to have appropriate 17th century costumes and dances, the music interpolated is either an irrelevant piece of any old baroque concerto or a completely inauthentic pastiche by a modern composer. Audiences are thus deprived of an integral element of the play and Purcell's songs are confined to the concert hall and records where, separated from the scenes they were meant to accompany, they only make half the sense they should.

Chapter 8

From Sickness to Fly in Vain

In January 1694 Purcell had his first and only opportunity to have a work premièred outside England. There were centenary celebrations on 9th for the refounding of Trinity College, Dublin by Queen Elizabeth, though in the twentieth century the College chose to commemorate the event in 1992. Since Nahum Tate was a graduate of Trinity and Poet Laureate (the first Irishman to hold the post) he was an obvious choice to write an appropriate ode. He obliged with *Great Parent, Hail,* scored for the forces that Purcell could have expected to be available in the Irish capital; the instrumentalists from the Theatre Royal (who are likely to have been familiar with Purcell's music for the plays), the choirs of Christ Church and St Patrick's Cathedrals and the competent musicians among the students and staff. The men of the choirs would have known Purcell's music too, possibly from his anthems but extensively from his catches, which could have been enjoyed at The Hibernian Catch Club, formed by them 14 years before.

Sadly Purcell himself did not attend. He only had two official excuses to leave the island of Britain during his life – the trip to the Netherlands with the King in 1690 and the performance of his ode in Dublin – but on neither occasion was he able to do so. For him and his family the weeks around Christmas 1693 were hectic. As well as the birth of the baby and the composition for Dublin, Purcell was moving house; this time to Marsham Street, only a few yards from the old house in Bowling Alley East where his wife's family now lived. The Purcells themselves seem to have

Trinity College, Dublin. Purcell wrote an Ode for its centenary.

moved out of Westminster for the previous two years. Although we do not know where to, it has been plausibly suggested by Maureen Duffy that they lived in Chelsea, either at or near Priest's school, where Purcell could teach his expanding list of pupils with minimal disruption yet still reach the various royal residences with ease. However, against this, Dorset Garden Theatre was quite a long haul down the river at a time when Purcell was needed there more often than ever. The Priests lived close to Lindsey House, at the southern limit of old Chelsea, and the theatre was at Blackfriars. It was either a long row or an expensive carriage ride.

On 25 January there was the concert at York Buildings of his music, at which *Hail, Bright Cecilia* was given its third performance. The occasion was the state visit of Prince Lewis of Baden, one of William's most valued allies in the year's campaign against the French. At the beginning of the month it also seems that Purcell wrote another ode especially for the visit; a setting of verses by Matthew Prior, *Light of the World,* to be performed either at Kensington or Whitehall. However the music is lost, although the printed version of the text published at the time says that Purcell did set it.

In the theatre, January saw a rather sad event when Dryden, by now disillusioned and none too well, announced his retirement from writing for the stage, bowing out with a tragicomedy, *Love Triumphant,* or *Nature Will Prevail.* Unfortunately, the only thing that proved to be triumphant was the title. Unlike D'Urfey, whom Dryden had accused of it the year before, the old poet had lost his touch. As was increasingly the case, the exclusive understanding between Anne Bracegirdle and John Eccles meant that Purcell had to share the musical honours and only had one song to write. He had scarcely more to do when Thoms Southerne turned his hand to tragedy the next month. His work, *The Fatal Marriage,* one of the most effective tear-jerkers of the period, needed two songs. In April, however, he provided a full instrumental suite as well as the song 'See Where Repenting Celia Lies' for *The Married Beau*, or *The Curious Impertinent* by John Crowne, who Dryden used mischievously to infer was his illegitimate half-brother, although Crowne had been born in the New World and educated at Harvard.

That April too Purcell composed the greatest of his works for Queen Mary during her lifetime, the astonishing ode *Come, Ye Sons of Art Away.* This work includes the duet 'Sound the

Trumpet' for two counter-tenors – perhaps himself included at that first performance – in which high male voices imitate trumpets to such thrilling effect that no real brass are needed. In many senses the ode, with its constant references to the character of musical instruments, is a continuation of the subject matter in *Hail, Bright Cecilia* but the confidence and sheer virtuosity of the writing for strings, oboes and trumpets lifts its splendours onto an even higher plain. This is music to be felt physically as much as admired. The stately overture is emphatic yet almost melancholy, a mood dispelled with a tune of exuberant majesty for the words of the title. 'Strike the Viol,' which follows, has a lilting accompaniment that swings between the instruments almost as a motum perpetuum. The way Purcell allows the chorus to pick up the verses of the soloists in other movements anticipates Handel's oratorio writing in the middle of the next century.

Why Purcell should have been so moved to write an ode of such extraordinary power that year is a mystery. Perhaps it was because it was the fifth anniversary of the coronation and for the first time in three springs William was able to attend. It was for Mary's thirty-second birthday and because William was on the continent for most of the year – referred to in the bass solo, 'These Are The Sacred Charms That Shield Her Hero In The Field' – she had had sole executive authority for much longer than she ever intended. D'Urfey's comparison of her to Queen Elizabeth in *The Yorkshire Feast Ode* was becoming fulfilled. She was the most powerful woman in England or Scotland for a hundred years. With everybody but her sister Anne, with whom she was no longer on speaking terms, she had acted with firmness and diplomacy. Although Mary had had an uncomfortable bout of fever, probably flu, and was (as many do at the same age) complaining that she was beginning to feel old, as far as the public were concerned she was in excellent health. She had gained the respect, as well as the affection, of her subjects in a way achieved by no other Stuart monarch. The cool administrative government of William and his ability to step aside from the internal conflicts of English politics had done more to calm the religious, economic and social turmoil of 50 years than was recognised at the time. But for all his bravery and efficiency, he was never a man to inspire great music. For Mary, Purcell at his sixth attempt fashioned one of the world's most wonderful and enduring birthday presents. It was to be her last.

Purcell was paired with John Eccles again for the major theatrical score of the season, the first two parts of D'Urfey's

The Comical History of Don Quixote. This was a very free adaptation of Cervantes' novel and it opened in May. The episodes gave plenty of opportunity for music, including famous mad songs from both composers. Purcell supplied the baritone John Bowman with six minutes of extremely difficult but effective rantings in 'Let the Dreadful Engines.' Eccles gave Anne Bracegirdle 'I Burn, My Brain Consumes to Ashes,' in part two of the play; a piece of casting which would have been seen as a neat reversal of her usual roles and indeed of her attitude in the first half of the plot. Then, with yet more references by D'Urfey to her as the cause of Mountfort's death, she plays the unconcerned mourner at the funeral of an unrequited lover. In part two it is she that is maddened by rejected love. The first evening ended with a peculiar and somewhat macabre masque in which Don Quixote looks set to be burned alive to Purcell's jolly music. From the composer's point of view the high point of the second evening was the rousing 'trumpet song', 'The Genius of England.' It was given extra contemporary spice by the fact that it was sung by Catherine Cibber, daughter of the King's Sergeant Trumpeter, Matthew Shore and sister of John Shore for whom Purcell had written his recent spectacular trumpet obliggatos and who accompanied her at the first performances. *Don Quixote* was not as much of a challenge as the previous semi-operas had been. However, given that the company was in almost as disastrous a financial position as the old patent companies had been 15 years before, it was a valuable opportunity to keep the taste for large-scale theatrical music alive.

The discrepancy in the reputations of Eccles and Purcell now makes it seem strange that they shared the work. But Eccles was a highly gifted theatrical songwriter in his own way, often better suited to the actors than Purcell, whose musical demands were simply too hard. And Purcell's preference for writing for the professional singers, even though he wrote plenty of easier pieces that non-specialists outside the theatre could sing, meant that many of the company's star players were not prepared or able to tackle his songs. There was also the old English tradition of including songs by several composers in the same entertainment. This trait developed into the ballad opera in the next century and lingers on even now in pantomime. On any one evening, this ranged from the multiple contributions from Matthew Locke, Pelham Humfrey, John Banister and Pietro Reggio in the music for Shadwell's version of *The Tempest* to the plays of the nineties where Purcell

The contract, countersigned by Purcell, for Bernard Smith's rebuilding of the Westminster Abbey organ.

was only one of several musicians – including sometimes D'Urfey and Shadwell themselves – whose songs were heard.

During the summer of 1694 work was begun on rebuilding the Westminster Abbey organ. Bernard Smith, with whom Purcell had worked on instruments for the Temple Church and St Catherine's Cree, was asked to extend the range of the organ by four stops but otherwise to use the same pipes and casing. The complications involved are indicated by the fact that the Abbey authorities allowed £200 for the work (which can be compared with the £40 Purcell had needed to put the Chapel Royal organ into good order seven years before) and expected it to take until November 1695. Purcell, as organist and an experienced instrument-maker himself, supervised the improvements.

Purcell was becoming known as a first rate teacher as well as a performer and composer. His pupils ranged from the daughters of aristocratic patrons like the Howards – who were expected to be highly accomplished in music to a degree which would now make them semi-professional – to boys at the Chapel Royal. Young musicians like John Weldon and Jeremiah Clarke both wrote works which did their teacher great credit. Poor Clarke, who eventually committed suicide over a love affair, for years had his most famous composition, the *Trumpet Voluntary*, attributed to Purcell. There seems to have been an endearing modesty about Purcell as a teacher which made him much loved by his students, whatever their level. He taught seven-year-olds the keyboard as well as teaching senior students composition. Some lived in his house (or his mother-in-law's house) in Westminster, some came to him every day for a lesson, some were tutored more occasionally. Much of the philosophy he passed on to his pupils we know from the *Introduction to the Skill of Musick*. Originally by John Playford, it was Purcell who revised the work extensively for its 1694 edition. His views follow those which were already clear from the prefaces to his published works and the music itself. He heaps lavish praise on Italian music and recommends it as a guide, as he does the works of his friend, colleague and own teacher, John Blow. Most importantly, however, he argues against rigid rules, calling instead for harmonic and melodic freedom to give the music 'air'. Discords he asserts, can be more interesting than harmonically perfect chords which can become 'cloying' and warns against 'nice rules' in counterpoint. It is indeed good advice. It is Purcell's cheerful delight in breaking the rules at the right

A receipt from Purcell of £2 rent.

moment which gives his music its zest and individuality at a time when too much of what was being written became unidentifiable as anything other than generally pleasant baroque.

Once again in 1694 he was called upon to contribute to the St Cecilia celebrations. Instead of writing an ode for the feast and concert in Stationer's Hall as he had done two years previously, however, he brought new splendour to the service in St Bride's, Fleet Street, which traditionally preceded it. For this he called on all his combined experience of anthem writing for the Chapel Royal and laudatory odes to write the first ever setting in English of the *Te Deum* and *Jubilate* to have full orchestral accompaniment. Yet again London was stunned by Purcell's sheer daring and the exuberance of his ceremonial writing. Thomas Tudway, the organist of King's College, Cambridge, who had known Purcell as a boy at the Chapel Royal, later wrote that it was these works more than any other which raised his reputation above those of his contemporaries. 'I dare challenge,' he went on, 'all the Orators, Poets, Painters &c of any Age whatsoever, to form so lively an Idea of Choirs of Angels singing, & paying their Adorations.' After nearly 300 years it is not a judgement that needs much revision. Purcell worked on the *Te Deum* and *Jubilate* through the autumn and they were performed on 22 November, with a repeat for the King and Queen on 9 December. The two works were published in 1697 by Frances Purcell after they had been used at the opening service of Wren's new St Paul's Cathedral. They then became an integral part of the annual Sons of the Clergy festival there for most of the 18th century, alternating each year with Handel's great *Te Deums*, the *Utrecht* and *Dettingen*.

In the meantime the King had returned from the campaigns in Flanders that had kept him out of the country since the beginning of May and Purcell wrote a short anthem, *The Way of God is an Undefiled Way*, to welcome him home on 11 November. As well, the string of theatre commissions continued with pieces for a revival of Dryden's *Tyrannic Love* and Edward Ravenscroft's *The Canterbury Guests*. But by now the company was falling apart as the rows between Betterton and the company manager, Christopher Rich, became increasingly bitter. Rich, a lawyer by training, which did nothing to endear him to the actors, had in 1690 bought the patent that Charles D'Avenant had inherited from his father. For what amounted to total control of two theatres and England's state company, he paid the grand sum of £80. Rich was loathed and regarded as interested in nothing but a commercial return. In his defence it must be said that for the first few years it was his financial acumen combined with Betterton's artistic judgement which so spectacularly revived the company after the difficult years of the 1680s.

Nonetheless the extravagance of the semi-operas and the occasional failure of new plays had taken their toll and by December 1694 Rich took the traditional measures of management in a crisis. He cut the actors wages and reduced the roles of the senior and more expensive players, giving their parts to new and untested, but much cheaper, performers. They appealed to the Lord Chamberlain, who, as controller of the royal household, was their ultimate boss. A week before Christmas he asked the venerable Sir Robert Howard, Dryden's brother-in-law, to arbitrate. More serious events, however, soon made the squabbles seem irrelevant.

It had been a wet summer and small-pox had flared up in an outbreak that was beginning to cause great alarm. Hundreds were dying each week in an epidemic that was soon the worst to hit London since the plague 30 years before. On 22 December Queen Mary was unwell and it soon became clear that she had the disease. She seems to have been certain that she was going to die from the first sign, hurriedly making her will, sorting her papers and reconciling herself to death. William, who had been away for so much of their joint reign and whose bisexual affairs were beginning to cause the sort of scandal that had accompanied Charles II, was nonetheless deeply fond of Mary and was desperate to save her. So was the government. Mary had managed it well and there was alarm at the prospect of the political turmoil that could be caused if William was in sole charge and yet spending half the year personally leading his troops into battle on the continent. There was, though, little to be done. Many people had small-pox and survived. However the strain of 1694 seems to have been particularly virulent and the doctors had no more answer to the disease than they had to most others. As usual they resorted to useless bleeding of the patient and a few soothing herbs. Mary was dead in six days.

When her uncle Charles had died ten years before he was buried in Westminster Abbey in a quiet funeral rather than a great state occasion. Perhaps because she was so young, or perhaps because she had been such a stabilising force on the country which people were desperately anxious not to lose, it

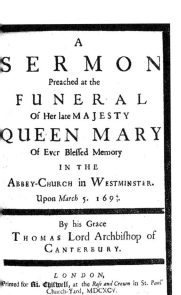

A
SERMON
Preached at the
FUNERAL
Of Her late MAJESTY
QUEEN MARY
Of Ever Bleſſed Memory
IN THE
ABBEY-CHURCH in WESTMINSTER.
Upon *March* 5. 169⅘.

By his Grace
THOMAS Lord Archbiſhop of
CANTERBURY.

LONDON,
Printed for Ri. Chiſwell, at the *Roſe and Crown* in St. Paul'
Church-Yard, MDCXCV.

he Sermon for Queen Mary's
ineral three month's after
er death: a much more lavish
eremony than she had
nvisaged.

was decided to give Mary a full state funeral and postpone it until the beginning of March 1695. In the meantime her body was embalmed and laid in state in Whitehall Palace. The epidemic and a winter of exceptional severity made it a miserable time for many. The theatres closed and public mourning for Mary seems somehow to have acted as a focus for the fears of the whole city. She was mourned in Holland too, where she had made her home before becoming Queen. According to John Evelyn, £50,000 was spent on the funeral procession and Abbey ceremony. Too late a paper was found in one of Mary's closets asking that her body should 'not be opened, or any extraordinary expense at her funeral'.

Two Sackbuts, and a Double Courtall

Musicians in procession playing sakbutts and a double courtall, or curtal, an early instrument similar in tone to the bassoon.

Exactly what music of Purcell's was played before and during the service in Westminster Abbey has been speculated about for the last 250 years. The accounts that survive, particularly by Thomas Tudway, tell us that there were drums muffled by black velvet which accompanied the procession, itself draped in black cloaks and moving between buildings shrouded in the same way. Purcell reworked the *Funeral Sentences* he had written originally as an apprentice and revised once already in the early 1680s. To these he added the march heard in *The Libertine*. From it he also fashioned a canzona for flatt trumpets, which had slides like sackbuts (or modern trombones) except that they extended behind the player's shoulder. The conductor Robert King has argued convincingly, both in his book on Purcell and in performance, that the march and canzona could not have been accompanied by the side and kettle drums as they are on most modern recordings, wonderfully effective as it is. There was then no tradition of drums, which were strictly military instruments, in the Abbey and he argues that unloading them from the processional horses and setting them up would have been impractical. Equally it was impossible to play the flatt trumpets while moving. The march would thus have sounded as it does in *The Libertine* music; stark and devoid of embellishment as the coffin was brought up the nave of the Abbey. The drums would have been sounded on their own as the coffin progressed through the streets of Westminster. Before the burial itself in Henry VII's Chapel the choir sang the *Funeral Sentences,* which are quite devastating. The poignancy of Purcell's setting of the words 'He fleeth as it were a shadow' at the start of the first sentence, followed by the wrenchingly chromatic 'In the midst of life we are in death,' the second, is overwhelming. Towards the end of the service the choir sang the specially composed anthem *Thou Knowest Lord the Secrets of Our*

Hearts, now accompanied only by the mournful trumpets. Afterwards the mood was changed from agonised solemnity to the sad but more forward-looking music of the canzona, developed for the flatt trumpets from the earlier march. The end of the service was not the end of Purcell's tribute to Mary, though. In May, just after the moment when in previous years Mary would have had a birthday ode, Purcell and Blow published three elegies. Blow set verses beginning *No, No, Lesbia,* which Purcell then put into a Latin version, *Incassum Lesbia* for soprano solo, to which was added a duet, *O Dive Custos.*

For the first three months of the year the combination of a freezing winter, small-pox (which by January was claiming several hundred a week) and the official mourning for the Queen meant that London's normal life all but ground to a halt. Peter Motteaux gave up trying to keep *The Gentleman's Journal* afloat and the theatre remained closed. The hiatus did nothing to heal the rift between Betterton and Rich. Indeed it gave Betterton the opportunity to make plans of his own. He could argue that the United Company effectively had a monopoly that was not intended when King Charles issued two patents and so he requested permission to leave Rich at Drury Lane and Dorset Gardens and set up on his own. This he was allowed to do and so, by a fine irony, ended back where he had started with William D'Avenant 35 years before; renovating the old tennis court in Portugal Row, Lincoln's Inn Fields, yet again. With Betterton went many of the actors and singers who had made the United Company thrive: Thomas Doggett, John Bowman, Mrs. Ayliffe, Elizabeth Barry and, most damaging, Anne Bracegirdle. John Eccles and William Congreve inevitably went wherever she did. For posterity, perhaps the most inconvenient defection was that of John Downes, the prompter, who had been with Betterton since the Restoration and whose memoirs, *Roscius Anglicanus,* are the prime source of information about productions and dates at the patent theatres.

Purcell, however, did not join the rebel company, electing instead to stay with Christopher Rich, even if he was mean and unpleasant to work for. On the face of it this seems strange since it meant that he was left with very few experienced performers for his music, although Catherine Cibber remained, as did Susanna Percival, Mountfort's widow who had by then married another actor in the company, John Verbruggen. Instead he had to rely on singers like Letitia Cross, who was possibly not yet 14, and the even younger – though brilliant – treble, Jemmy Bowen.

Letitia Cross (1681-1725), who sang in most of the plays with music by Purcell in 1695. Portrayed by Kneller as St. Catherine.

But in many ways Purcell's decision – if he was required to make one: it is perfectly possible that Betterton did not ask him to join him – makes perfect sense. He was less interested in the writing of songs for actors than in the spectacular possibilities of the semi-operas. The Lincoln's Inn theatre was a fit-up job which had nothing like the technical possibilities for scenery at Dorset Gardens. Equally his relations with Betterton had never been exactly warm. All through the 1680s Purcell had been pretty much ignored at a time when the money and recognition would have meant a lot to the young composer. I think it quite likely that Betterton and Purcell had very different ideas of how music should be used in the theatre: Purcell believing it should accompany and comment on the action, Betterton wanting to hear it more integrated and simpler. In fact Purcell's real activity in the theatre coincided with Christopher Rich's buy-out of the company so it is possible that the enthusiasm for his work came from Rich, not primarily from Betterton. It was certainly Rich who had pushed the company towards more operatic productions, a trend which had always been fiercely resisted by the actors who felt that, however good their own voices, they would soon lose their positions to singers in the affections of the public; a fear that was seen to be fully justified when Handel and Bononcini brought Italian opera to the height of fashion 15 years later. The final consideration for Purcell would have been the two-sided opportunity offered by the defection of John Eccles. On one side it meant that he was cut off for good from some of his favourite and most trusted performers. On the other it meant that he would no longer have to share productions with Eccles whose music would have to be included as long as Anne Bracegirdle continued to sing. Purcell stayed where he was and Rich rewarded him with an astonishing volume of work.

Just what Purcell's absence from the stage in the 1680s meant was seen in the first production to use his music after the split. It was also his first chance to write music for a play by the leading woman playwright of the time, Aphra Behn, who had died in 1688. Her tragedy *Abdelazer: or The Moor's Revenge,* was staged in April. Purcell wrote the Overture, as well as an extremely difficult song for Jemmy Bowen, 'Lucinda is Bewitching Fair,' and several dances – among them the *Rondeau* that Benjamin Britten made famous (and used so brilliantly) when he adopted it as the theme for his set of variations, *The Young Person's Guide to the Orchestra*. Purcell, one feels, would have been amazed and delighted by the rousing power of a full modern orchestra playing his unassuming tune. Purcell paid a back-handed tribute to the rebel company soon afterwards when he set a lyric for the revival of Dryden's *The Spanish Fryar.* The two composers who had decamped with Betterton were Eccles and Godfrey Finger. Purcell therefore dedicated his song 'While I With Grief Did On You Look,' also sung by Bowen, to 'Mrs Bracegirdle Singing (I Burn &c [Eccles' mad song]) in ye play of *Don Quixote'.* Finger had just set the same lyric, with very much the same dedication. Purcell, it seems, was indulging in a game of 'anything you can do, I can do better'.

Purcell also still had the services of some of the best instrumentalists, like the trumpeter John Shore and the wind player James Paisible. The latter was a Frenchman who had lived in England for most of his adult life. As well as being recognised as a virtuoso on the recorder and oboe he was a composer who had written the music for a masque by John Crowne in the 1670s, the star of which was Mary Davis. Both he and the King were obviously impressed. She became Charles' mistress (and Blow's Venus) but after the King's death she married Paisible. He had also written the original dances for Shadwell's rewrite of *Timon of Athens* in 1678 which included a masque by Grabu. Replacing this, but not Paisible's dances, became Purcell's next project for Rich. His masque is an elegant interlude of nearly 20 minutes to entertain Timon at dinner in Act II. It demonstrated that the patent company intended to continue its large-scale musical presentations whatever the problems posed by defections. The *Timon* masque ends with a refrain for Cupid and Bacchus that shows Purcell at his lightest and most engaging; a mood that is caught in his catches, more than 30 of which Henry Playford included that year in the new volume of *The Pleasant Musical Companion:*

'Come, let us agree, there are pleasures divine
In wine and in love, in love and in wine.'

Purcell was a much-liked and often seen figure in the pubs of London, a good drinking companion to writers like Tom Brown, Robert Gould and of course Tom D'Urfey, who were known for the capacity of their livers as well as their satire and wit. Sadly war damage and the developer's hammer have meant that very few pubs from the 17th century have survived in central London and none in the area of Westminster where Purcell lived or down by the river where the Queen's Theatre stood.

In the summer of 1695 the overture to *Timon of Athens* was also used to begin the last ode that Purcell was to write for the royal family. *Who Can From Joy Refrain?* was composed for the youngest member, William, Duke of Gloucester, the son of Princess Anne and Prince George, who was now second in line to the throne. He celebrated his sixth birthday on 24 July at Kew, his mother's residence since she had been thrown out of Whitehall Palace five years before. The title was a genuine sigh of relief because it looked for a few days that spring as if young William would follow his aunt to the grave as a result of small-pox.

In August Purcell would have been at work on the theatre music for the autumn season. Rich, having lost so many of the best writers to Betterton, was relying on revivals but also beginning to cast around for new talent. One potential catch was Robert Gould, who had spent nine years as a servant in the household of the Duke of Dorset, but who was making a name for himself as a scathing wit. His attempts for the theatre were tragedies, the first of which, *The Rival Sisters: or, The Violence of Love*, was produced in the Theatre Royal in September or October. John Blow wrote some of the music but the major part was by Purcell; the overture and three songs included another for Jemmy Bowen, 'Celia Has a Thousand Charms'. Another newcomer was Thomas Scott, whose comedy *The Mock Marriage* seems to have been performed at about the same time. Purcell's songs for this, to lyrics by Motteux and D'Urfey, included two which became very popular; 'Man Is For the Woman Made' (which had to be sung by Letitia Cross – with wild improbability – because the actor Michael Lee could not sing it), and 'Twas Within a Furlong of Edinburgh Town', a Scots tune which is about as Scottish as Lilliburlero is Irish.

The autograph of part of the High Priest's invocation in Act V of *The Indian Queen*, Purcell's last major work for the stage, which was completed by his brother Daniel.

Letitia Cross also sang a song which Purcell added to the autumn's revival of Shadwell's version of *The Tempest*, 'Dear Pretty Youth.' She played Dorinda, Miranda's sister, in one of the superfluous episodes added to Shakespeare's original plot. Traditionally Purcell is said to have completely rewritten the old score compiled by Locke, Humfrey, Reggio and Banister and records are still issued with this attribution, presumably because Purcell's name is bound to sell and the music is too good not to be heard. Along with John Eccles' score for Congreve's *Semele* and *The Judgement of Paris* it blows apart the often repeated theory that there was no music composed for the London stage worth listening to between Purcell's death and Handel's arrival. It is much more likely, given the amount of time that Purcell had in the middle of 1695, that the new *Tempest* was in fact composed by his pupil John Weldon, whom he had finished teaching the year before, for a production in 1704. There are several good musicological reasons for thinking this – apart from anything else the music sounds much closer to that from Handel's generation than from Purcell's. It would have been quite probable that Weldon kept the one song by his mentor from the older version out of affection and respect.

There was an extended score, however, for the main crowd-puller of the early part of the season, an adaptation of John Fletcher's epic of Roman Briton and the Caractacus legend, *Bonduca*. Apart from the overture, one of his best, and various short dances, Purcell's main contribution was a long temple scene in Act III, which included a prayer to a pagan god who rejoiced in the name Rugwith. Perhaps it is hardly surprising that he turned out not to be the answer to the Britons' parlous position. Good as Purcell's music is, this is one Restoration rewrite which would now be unwatchable.

There was one more major score from Purcell, though exactly when it was written and performed is a mystery which has exasperated scholars for decades. We know that before the United Company's final internal row at the end of 1694 Rich had commissioned Betterton to refashion *The Indian Queen* by John Dryden and Sir Robert Howard, first staged 30 years earlier. It was to follow the pattern of *King Arthur* and *The Fairy-Queen* as a major operatic extravaganza for the spring. As before, Purcell was asked to provide the music. Perhaps it was because of the imminent production and his obvious interest in saving it that Howard was appointed the mediator between the actors and the management just before Queen Mary's death that Christmas. Betterton had made little progress on the adaptation by the time he and Rich parted company. Nonetheless a revised text was supplied, possibly by Dryden himself, which made room for a masque for Fame and Envy in Act II and more than 20 other separate musical items, including the famous song 'I Attempt From Love's Sickness to Fly.' These were set by Henry Purcell, while a complete masque to end the work was composed by his brother Daniel, who was moving back to London from his job at Magdalen College, Oxford. To accommodate the changes nearly half the lines from the original play had to be cut. When Betterton was given permission to move to Lincoln's Inn Fields in March it became clear that there could be no production of such a complicated piece that spring because so many of the vital members of the cast would no longer be available to The Queen's Theatre. The advantage of having only one major company in the country capable of mounting full scale music theatre was that the audience was not split. The disadvantage was that, unlike the days of D'Avenant, Jolly and Killigrew, there was no reservoir of trained talent to draw on in a crisis.

Purcell in a sketch by Kneller.

Quite how long the postponement was we do not know. But it seems certain that *The Indian Queen* was staged before the end of the year because some of the songs were published. The printer admitted the edition was unauthorised but implied that he did not think Purcell would mind. Therefore the composer must have been alive at the time and the songs must have been well enough known in the theatre to be worth pirating. It is possible that it could have been staged in late June, though that would have strained the company, especially green players like Cross, to their limits.

If *Bonduca* was given earlier in September, rather than October, and was followed in repertoire by *The Mock Marriage* and *The Rival Sisters*, then the most likely date for *The Indian Queen's* première is late October 1695. This would mean that either reasons for Daniel's participation – that Henry was already ill or that he was giving Daniel a brotherly leg-up in the profession on his return to London – could be valid. Henry's score has some of his finest writing for the stage, not only in wonderful songs like 'They Tell Us That Your Mighty Powers Above', but also in the act tunes and other instrumental numbers. *The Indian Queen* is a tragedy and Purcell, fresh from writing the music for Queen Mary's funeral, perhaps, catches moments of great poignancy. It must have been easy for audiences seeing the work in the months following Purcell's death to have seen it prefigured in what they heard.

I attempt from love's sickness to fly in vain
Since I am myself my own fever and pain.

For there was little time left for him. There was a duet of sexual awakening for Letitia Cross and Jemmy Bowen in Southerne's script of Aphra Behn's novel *Oroonoko*, premièred in early November. There was another great song for another very minor play; 'Sweeter than Roses' in Richard Norton's *Pausanias*, which may not have been performed until the following spring with the rest of the music taken over by Daniel. There was a final song for Princess Anne around the time of King William's birthday, 'Lovely Albina's Come Ashore.' Frances later wrote that this was the last lyric Henry wrote before he became ill.

Lastly, for his friend Tom D'Urfey and young Letitia Cross, in a production that was an embarrassing failure, the third part of *Don Quixote*, Purcell wrote 'From Rosy Bow'rs'. By that time he was seriously ill. Yet, great man of the theatre that he was, the song captures perfectly the fake threat of death for a girl pretending to be lovesick, not his own very serious fears. In the tortured harmonies that accompany the third section, though, he came close to revealing the real position:-

Cold despair,
Disguised like snow and rain,
Falls on my breast;
Bleak winds in tempests blow,
My veins all shiver
And my fingers glow;
My pulse beats a dead march
For lost repose,
And to a solid lump of ice
My poor, fond heart is froze.

It was the only song for the show he managed to write. Ralph Courtville and Thomas Morgan supplied most of the rest.

What had happened to take him from one of his busiest and most creative periods to his deathbed in a matter of a fortnight? It was not small-pox, it seems, which had killed so many during the year. Nor does it seem likely that Purcell was suffering from any long term condition which suddenly flared up, as was the case with Mozart who died at the same age, 36, so nearly a 100 years later. The story that was handed down by the Gostling family was that Frances was to blame. Apparently she had been infuriated by Purcell's habit of staying out late drinking with his friends and had ordered the servants not to let him in after midnight. They obeyed and when he arrived back at Marsham Street he found himself locked out. It was a damp and miserable November. He caught cold and the cold turned into something worse. Many musicologists balk at the account, finding any stories of loose living and unreasonable behaviour by either Purcell or his wife (who had seen many difficulties in their

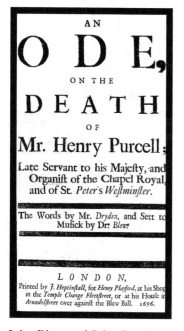

AN

ODE,

ON THE

DEATH

OF

Mr. Henry Purcell;

Late Servant to his Majesty, and
Organist of the Chapel Royal,
and of St. *Peter's Westminster.*

The Words by Mr. *Dryden*, and Sett to
Musick by Dr: *Blow.*

LONDON,
Printed by *J. Heptinstall*, for *Henry Playford*, at his Shop
in the *Temple Change Fleetstreet*, or at his House in
Arundelstreet over against the Blew Ball. 1696.

John Blow and John Dryden's
Ode to Purcell, performed in the
memorial concert in York
Buildings.

14 years of marriage) too damaging to the image of their hero to contemplate. The scholars would prefer a tidier end. So theories of tuberculosis have grown up which were certainly not current at the time and seem to have no basis in the working pattern of his life during the preceding months. It is far more likely that an infection turned to pneumonia or rheumatic fever. Whether Frances locked him out or not it is perfectly possible that, at a time when he must have been spending many night hours in the theatre or relaxing after performances (which had, after all, probably been how he had met Frances in the first place) he would wander home late through St James's Park. It does seem unlikely, though, that he sat shivering on the doorstep. He had plenty of friends from the Abbey and court nearby who would have given him shelter in an emergency. It was a robust age when the sight of the organist somewhat the worse for wear would not have been exactly shocking.

Whatever the cause, the result was disastrous. The usual pointless remedies, such as bleeding, were applied and probably reduced his resistance further. All through the third week of November he steadily lost ground. He was not by nature a pessimist, however, and it was only when it was clear that he was close to death, sometime during the day on 21 November, that he was prepared to make a will. It was witnessed by John Baptist Peters, his brother-in-law, William Eccles, a local apothecary, and John Chaplin, who lived close by.

'In the Name of God Amen I Henry Purcell of the Ciity of Westmr. Gentl. being dangerously Ille as to the Constitution of my Body But in good and perfect Mind and Memory (thanks bee to God) Doe by these presents publish & Declare this to bee my last Will & Testamt. And I doe hereby Give & bequeath unto my Loveing Wife Frances Purcell All my Estate both real & personall of what Nature and kind soever, to her & to her Assignes for Ever...'

A little while later, before he could see another St Cecilia's Day, he died.

In life Purcell had been honoured and respected to a remarkable degree for an artist who would nowadays be only just thought to be entering maturity at 36. In 1695 he was accorded more tributes at his death than any English musician had been before. He was buried in Westminster Abbey on 26 November, five days after he had died: not in the cloisters, where so many of his family – father, uncle and several children

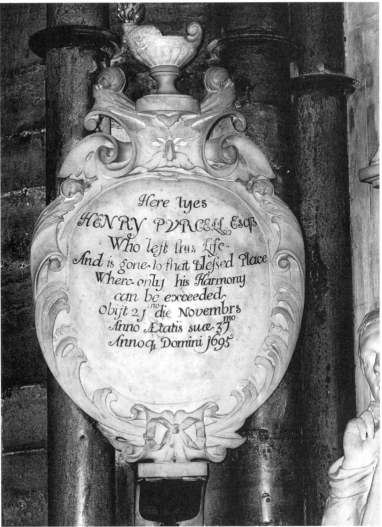

The monument to Purcell that hangs above his grave in Westminster Abbey; not in the cloisters like his father, uncle and children, but in the north aisle at the foot of the organ.

– lay already, but in the north aisle of the church itself, at the foot of the new organ which had been due for completion under his direction only three weeks before. All his colleagues from the Chapel Royal and the Abbey Choir attended, as did the Dean and full Chapter. In an extraordinary gesture they waived all the normal funeral charges. At the service the trumpeters joined the choirs for the second time in less than a year to perform Purcell's own march, sentences, anthem and canzona with which they had buried Queen Mary. John Blow, his teacher and closest musical friend, took over once again the organist's place he had relinquished nearly 20 years before.

A little while later there was a memorial concert in York Buildings. The range of the tributes written by the poets and

Purcell's fellow composers gives as good a picture as any of the regard in which he was held. His brother Daniel joined his favourite librettist Nahum Tate to write one of many odes, *A Gloomy Mist O'erspreads the Plains*. Godfrey Finger and James Talbot wrote one for the concert, as did more famously John Blow and John Dryden. Purcell's pupil Jeremiah Clarke offered the most lavish; *Come, Come Along* for full choral forces including a dirge for flatt trumpets that recalled Purcell's own. There were musical expressions of grief too by his old boyhood friend Henry Hall and the young Irish composer Thomas Morgan. On the gravestone in the Abbey a Latin epitaph was carved, which W.H. Cummings translated,

> Applaud so great a guest, celestial powers,
> Who now resides with you, but once was ours:
> Yet let invidious earth no more reclaim
> Her short-lived favourite and her chiefest fame,

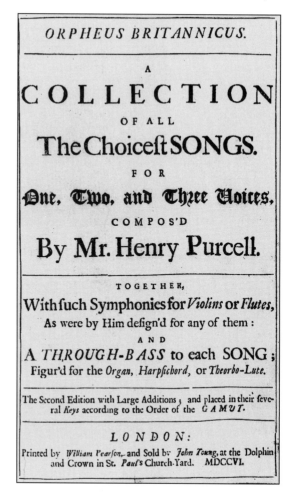

Complaining that so prematurely died
Good-nature's pleasure and devotion's pride.
Died? No, he lives, while yonder organs sound
And sacred echoes to the choir rebound.

In time the Howard family, several of whom were pupils and friends, arranged for a memorial to be fixed to the pillar in the Abbey near to where he is buried; it reads, 'Here lyes Henry Purcell Esq. Who left this life And is gone to that Blessed Place Where only his Harmony can be exceeded.'

During the following years Frances Purcell and Henry Playford published many of his chamber works which were not in print, culminating in the two volumes of the songs, *Orpheus Britannicus,* in 1698 and 1702. It was an inspired title which has stuck to Purcell's memory ever since. Frances herself moved to Richmond and died in 1706, probably in her early forties. Their two surviving children must have been hit hard by their father's death. Young Frances was seven and Edward was six. Edward lived until 1740 and was one of the founders of the Royal Society of Musicians. He and his wife Anne had a son, Edward Henry, who carried on the family tradition becoming a child of the Chapel Royal and an organist. Frances married a minor poet, Leonard Welstead, in 1707 but in 1726 died, like her father, at the age of 36.

London was right to mourn Purcell with such emotion. It was to be two hundred years before an English composer, Elgar, would appear who could be regarded as comparable with the best of other European contemporaries. Henry Hall was nearer the mark than he might have hoped when he ended his ode with,

Sometimes a Hero in an age appears,
But once a Purcell in a Thousand Years.

Dryden too recognised the reality of what they had lost and advised Purcell's fellow composers that they might as well stop;

Ye Brethren of the Lyre, and tunefull Voice,
Lament his lott: but at your own rejoyce.
Now live secure and linger out your days,
The Gods are pleas'd alone with Purcell's Layes,
Nor know to mend their Choice.

Further Reference

Felix Barker and Francis Jackson. **2000 Years Of London,** *London, 1974.*

Walter Besant. **Westminster,** *London, 1907.*

Jeremy Black and Jeremy Gregory (eds.). **Culture, Politics And Society In Britain 1660-1800,** *Manchester, 1991.*

Eric Blom. **Music In England,** *London, 1947 edition.*

Arthur Bryant. **Restoration England,** *London, 1960.*

E.J. Burford. **London, The Synfulle Citie,** *London, 1990.*

Sir George Clark. **The Later Stuarts 1660-1714,** *Oxford, 1932.*

Christopher Cook and John Wroughton. **English Historical Facts 1603-1688,** *London, 1980.*

W.H. Cummings. **Purcell,** *London, 1903.*

Arthur Dasent. **Nell Gwynne,** *London, 1924.*

Godfrey Davies. **The Early Stuarts 1603-1660,** *Oxford, 1959.*

Edward J. Dent. **Foundations Of English Opera,** *Cambridge, 1928.*

John Dryden. **Poems And Fables (ed. James Kinsley),** *Oxford, 1958.*

Maureen Duffy. **The Passionate Shepherdess, Aphra Behn, 1640-89,** *London, 1989 edition.*

Maureen Duffy. **Henry Purcell,** *London, 1994.*

Robert Elkin. **The Old Concert Rooms Of London,** *London, 1955.*

John Evelyn. **Diary (ed. William Bray, 1818), rev. edition,** *London, 1952.*

Antonia Fraser. **Charles II,** *London, 1993.*

Clement Antrobus Harris. **The Story Of British Music,** *London, c. 1920.*

John Harris, Stephen Orgel and Roy Strong. **The King's Arcadia: Inigo Jones And The Stuart Court,** *London, 1973.*

Geoffrey Holmes (ed.). **Britain After The Glorious Revolution 1689-1714,** *London, 1969.*

Imogen Holst (ed.). **Henry Purcell: Essays On His Music,** *London, 1959.*

Elizabeth Howe. **The First English Actresses: Women And Drama 1660-1700,** *Cambridge, 1992.*

Michael Hunter. **Science And Society In Restoration England,** *Cambridge, 1981.*

Arthur Hutchings. **Purcell,** *London, 1982.*

J.R. Jones. **The Revolution Of 1688 In England,** *London, 1972.*

J.R. Jones. **The Restored Monarchy 1660-1688,** *London, 1979.*

J.P. Kenyon. **The Stuarts,** *London, 1958.*

Robert King. **Henry Purcell,** *London, 1994.*

Robert Etheridge Moore. **Henry Purcell And The Restoration Theatre,** *London, 1961.*

Allardyce Nicoll. **British Drama (fifth edition),** *London, 1962.*

Roger North. **Essays On Music (ed. John Wilson),** *London, 1959.*

David Ogg. **England In The Reign Of Charles II,** *Oxford, 1956.*

Samuel Pepys. **Diary (ed. Lord Braybrooke, 1825),** *London, 1903.*

Curtis A. Price. **Henry Purcell And The London Stage,** *Cambridge, 1984.*

Sandra Richards. **The Rise Of The English Actress,** *London, 1993.*

David Thomas. **William Congreve,** *London, 1992.*

G.R.R. Treasure. **Seventeenth Century France,** *London, 1981.*

G.M. Trevelyan. **England Under The Stuarts, revised edition,** *London, 1925.*

Sir Jack Westrup. **Purcell,** *London, 1965.*

Franklin B. Zimmerman. **Henry Purcell,** *New York, 1967.*

Index

of persons, compositions, plays, places and events.
References to illustrations are in **bold** type.
Entries in *italic* type refer to plays, musical compositions and publications.